# The Logic of a Rose

## of a

# Rose

### Chicago Stories

For Kevin –

that you may find some
bit of truth, love, perhaps
beauty in these pages

Billy Lombardo

# The Logic
## of a
# Rose
### Chicago Stories

Billy Lombardo

Winner of the G. S. Sharat Chandra
Prize for Short Fiction
Selected by Gladys Swan

BkMk Press
University of Missouri-Kansas City

BkMk Press
University of Missouri-Kansas City
5101 Rockhill Road
Kansas City, Missouri 64110
(816)-235-2558 (voice); (816) 235-2611 (fax)
bkmk@umkc.edu/www.umkc.edu/bkmk

Cover design: Martin Z. Hernandez
Author photo: Ruth Hutton
Book interior design: Susan L. Schurman
Managing Editor: Ben Furnish
Printing: Walsworth Publishing Co., Marceline, Missouri

BkMk Press wishes to thank Bill Beeson, Heather Clark, Paul Tosh,
Jennifer Echavarria, Adriana Arteaga, special thanks to Karen I. Johnson.

The G. S. Sharat Chandra Prize for Short Fiction wishes to thank
Lindsey Martin-Bowen, Sandra K. Davies, Leslie Koffler, Elizabeth Smith

Library of Congress Cataloging-in-Publication Data

Lombardo, Billy
The logic of a rose: Chicago stories / Billy Lombardo
p. cm.
"Winner of G. S. Sharat Chandra Prize for Short Fiction."
ISBN 1886157502 (pbk.:alk.paper) 1. Chicago (Ill.)—Fiction.
2. Italian Americans—Fiction.
3. Italian American families—Fiction.
4. Young men—Fiction. 5. Catholics—Fiction.
6. Boys—Fiction. I. Title.

PS3612.O45L64 2005
813'.6—dc22                              2005004569

This book is set in Calisto type.
Second printing, 2005

For Elisa, my wife,
and for Seth and Kane, my sons,
without whom nothing makes much sense.

# Acknowledgments

Grateful acknowledgment is made to the editors of the periodicals in which these stories have appeared:

*Bryant Literary Review:* "The Hills of Laura"
*Cicada:* "The Thing about Swing," "Mrs. Higgins's Heart and the Smell of Fire," "The Wallace Playlot," and "The Pilgrim Virgin"
*Other Voices:* "The Hills of Laura" as "Something True"
*River Oak Review:* "The Pilgrim Virgin," "Blessed the Fruit"
*StoryQuarterly:* "Nickels"

The author would like to express gratitude to the Illinois Arts Council for awards that made it a little easier to write, and to the Ragdale Foundation for a fellowship he would certainly have taken them up on were it not for Little League baseball.

Thanks to Marc Smith who made a stage for a kid to mess up on, and Stuart Dybek who smiled when I told him I lived above Dressel's Bakery, which would have been enough. Thanks to Anne Calcagno, who made me feel like a writer; Debby Vetter of *Cicada* magazine, who did more for me than she can imagine; Mickie Flanagan for her generosity and friendship, at whose house in Aspen many of these stories began; Fred Shafer, Eric Davis, Billy Joel, Adam Davis, Tony Bennett, L'Tanya Evans, Tony Romano, Henry Sampson, Sandy Koufax, Dean Hacker, Charlie Puffer, and Marylee MacDonald, who helped me with the shape of these stories; Carie Lovstad, whose friendship and support have been great in value. Thanks to Ben Furnish, Susan Schurman, Karen Johnson, Gladys Swan, and the many eyes and heads and hands at BkMk Press. Thanks to A. Tom Bower (Wundy), who made it seem like there was some truth in most of the things I said; to Ruth Hutton for her friendship and a head shot; to Alice Price, Shelley Greenwood, Frank Hogan, Terry Pyer, Tamara Fraser, and the rest of my colleagues at The Latin School of Chicago, especially the librarians, who made a bigger deal out of me than I deserved; to Matty Vaccarello, my friend for life, and a bunch of Lombardos and former Lombardos who believed: Joe and Irene, Donna Jean, Jeffrey, Joe, Steve, Nini, and Johnny; and finally, thanks to Elisa, Seth, and Kane.

One of the major excitements of good fiction is to be drawn into an unfamiliar world and for a time to live there with complete absorption. It can be the Lower East Side of Bernard Malamud or the rural Georgia of Flannery O'Connor, the London of Dickens or the Australian landscape of Patrick White. Whatever it is, a good writer possesses the power to make that world come alive, to convince us of its reality and imaginative truth, and we leave it with the sense of refreshment and enlarged experience. Billy Lombardo's world is the Italian neighborhood of Bridgeport in Chicago, and his imaginative recreation of it is wonderfully evocative, convincing and appealing.

We enter his world through the eyes of Petey, a boy of eight, who begins his working life in Dressel's Bakery encouraged in the direction of hard work and integrity by his father. The stories advance through Petey's coming of age, but they follow the familiar coming-of-age track with great freshness and originality. Lombardo is particularly effective in capturing the emotional textures of experience—the tenderness of a neighbor toward Petey's mother after the fire; Petey's reception by his classmates after that event; Petey's tentative movements toward Rosalie and his response to her birthmark. Lombardo recreates not only the neighborhood with its bakery, the family apartment above it, the Romanos' garden, and the Wallace playlot, where boyhood is played out. He also recreates those who inhabit that milieu and share in the life there: those who run the bakery; Petey's father and mother; Mrs. Romano, the punk, and Bertie, and Rosalie. It is a fine collection of stories; I was delighted to enter Lombardo's world.

—Gladys Swan
Final Judge
G. S. Sharat Chandra Prize for Short Fiction

The Logic
of a
Rose
Chicago Stories

# Contents

# Nickels

I awoke to the swish of my father's slippers whispering *esses* across the kitchen floor. Water hissed into the sink, the old pipes clanged under the floors, the coffee tin clinked, and the spade of the scoop sunk into the coffee. The percolator bubbled. These were the Saturday sounds of my father getting ready for his weekend delivery job for the bakery downstairs.

When he passed the open sliver of my bedroom door, I kicked at the bed sheets, which had twisted around my feet in the night. I swung my legs to the floor, and followed him to the living room window. He was a shadow against the rectangle of glass and morning sun. I am certain he didn't know I was there, or that I was even awake. Had he known I'd just crossed from the dining room into the living room, he would not have cursed.

"Fuckin' punk," is what he said, and I froze between the two rooms, not sure for a second if the shadow was even my father.

Though we'd just moved into the third floor apartment above Dressel's Bakery, we had always lived in Bridgeport, which is to say, I'd heard the f-word before. If it had been at all possible, my father would've protected me from it. If he could have seen to it that people kept their mouths shut when they had nothing good to say, he would have done so, but he couldn't, and the shock of it now was that he'd used the word himself. I felt I'd done something wrong just to hear it.

I took tiny steps back to my room. In the old apartment I couldn't get up to pee in the middle of the night without the squeak of the floorboards waking my mother, but I didn't know this floor. With each step I expected a creak to betray me, but it never came. I reached my room and sat at the edge of my bed, mouthing the words my father had used. "Fuckin' punk." From the start of it at my lips to the end of it at the back of my throat the words used up my whole mouth. They were hard and quick and my father must have been pretty sore to say them.

I jiggled the doorknob and cleared my throat so that this time he'd hear me coming, and he turned around at the window. He held the curtain aside, and I slipped into the space under his arm and rubbed my eyes. Even then it seemed he didn't know I was there.

The morning light was easy. Kitty corner from the bakery below stood Joe Harris Hardware. There was a great big clock above the entrance; the face of it was a cartoon of Mr. Harris chewing on the stub of a green cigar. He owned the hardware store and the apartments above it, and the bakery building, too, but when you looked at him up there, pointing a short paintbrush at the hour and a long one at the minute, it seemed like he was in charge of time, too.

But my father was not looking at the clock. On the street below us, Gus Valenti sat on a yellow station wagon facing the Wallace Playlot. He held a cigarette in his hand, his fingers and thumb in the shape of OK. His brown hair covered the sloping collar of his dago-tee. He spit through his teeth between drags, and looked at his cigarette as he smoked, as if counting the drags he had left. When the red glow of it finally burned close to his fingertips, he took a long, deep drag, and with the smoke still in his lungs, he flicked the butt into the street. He was a lefty. He blew out smoke like he was angry at it.

My father squeezed the curtain in his fist. Across my back I felt the twitching muscles of his forearm, and I braced myself against another swearing.

"You know how old that punk is, Petey?" he asked. "Fifteen," he answered. "Fifteen years old." He stood at a hard angle above me, and his hair was rich and black. He spoke through closed teeth.

"You know whose car he's sitting on?" he said. "That's the baker's car," and he looked at me as though he was certain I understood. "Mr. Augle's been up since three o'clock in the morning, working his fingers to the bone in the bakery, and that lazy punk's just sitting on his car."

He said nothing about Gus smoking, nothing about him flicking his cigarette butts in the street, as if he expected the badness of those things to be obvious, and the lesson for me, here, was that being fifteen and lazy and sitting on Mr. Augle's car were the sins I needed to avoid.

"C'mon, Petey," he said. "Let's get you some coffee." He swung me around toward the kitchen, and I felt the weight of his arm as we walked.

We passed my bedroom door and I looked inside at the secret it kept of my father swearing. When we reached the kitchen, I laughed at the surprise of the linoleum floor my father and mother had installed during the night. It was white, gold sparkles sprinkling across it like fallen stars. It was so new I wondered for a moment if we might be rich. I looked up at my father.

"What do you think?" he said.

"It's great, Dad."

I started to pull a chair from the kitchen table, but he stopped me.

"Let me get it, Petey," he said. "Careful. Lift and pull, so as not to scrape the floor."

I sat with my chin in my hands, and my father kissed me on the cheek. He shaved every morning, even on weekends. His face was smooth and blue-gray and smelled like cream. At the counter he poured coffee into two cups, to mine he added sugar and a half-cup of milk. On his way toward me he stopped to consider a bubble in the linoleum with the toe of his slipper, biting his teeth together at the flaw, and I wondered if he wanted to swear again. It wasn't yet six in the morning, and he'd been disappointed twice.

"Listen," he said. "Promise me you won't grow up to be like that punk out there." Holding his cup, he returned to the bubble and began to worry it again.

I was going to be fifteen one day, but I promised anyway.

"Good boy," he said, shaking his head at the bubble. "I'm gonna miss you on my deliveries today," he said. "You ready for your first day on the job?"

Mr. Harris had hired me to sweep and mop the hallways of the bakery apartments.

I nodded, took a sip of coffee.

"Make sure you start at the top floor," he said. "And move from the back to the front as you mop."

"I know, Dad."

We'd been through the floor plan, as he called it, a million times that week. He'd worked it out so I wouldn't have to carry the bucket of water from floor to floor, and the night before, we'd even rehearsed with a broom and a dry mop. We walked up and down the hallway while he reminded me how to sweep, how to soak the mop, how to double up the strings of the mop in the wringer for maximum dehydration.

He circled his finger around the rim of his coffee cup. "Use plenty of water," he reminded me. "Prime solvent. Get the mop good and wet and drag it over the whole floor. Let it sit there a while to loosen the dirt." He sipped again. "After the water works into the floor, you wring it out for the once-over. The once-over absorbs most of the dirty water, and the twice-over picks up the rest. Remember what I said about the stroke?"

I nodded.

"Side to side as you walk backwards." He set his coffee cup down, and stood across the table from me, and holding an imaginary mop in his hands, he marched backwards. A mopless mime, he hummed "Love Makes the World Go Round," and made dreamy faces like he was dancing with an impossibly skinny girl—the swish of his slippers like music.

He stopped and finished his coffee.

"Pull the dirt toward you, right? Not up and back like they do in the movies. All that does is push the dirt around."

What he meant by "the movies" was *Mutiny on the Bounty*. We were watching it the Sunday before, and he'd said, "Petey, Petey, Petey..." loud and fast like I was going to miss something important if I didn't look right away. "Take a look at that guy swabbing the deck, there," he said. "I guarantee you that goofy actor's never mopped a floor in his life."

Each time he spoke to me about sweeping and mopping that week, he'd turned the discussion to what it meant to do a job well.

"You work hard for the guy who's paying you," he'd say. "You make him happy to have you working for him. You work so hard, that when he looks at you he can only think of how he's not paying you enough. And if you think he's paying an unfair wage, well, you continue to work hard, and you line yourself up another job, and you give him two weeks' notice, and you thank him for the opportunity to work for him. And then you work hard for two more weeks–you don't burn your bridges, see? You quit on a Friday, and start your new job on Monday."

To hear him talk about work was to believe it was true—as if it were work, after all, that made the world go around.

He washed his coffee cup in the sink and set it upside down on the drying rack. I was pretty sure he'd finished making his point about mopping, so I asked when they were planning on pouring the cement out front. Workers had ripped up the old concrete around the bakery, framing the corner with old lumber into the skeleton of a sidewalk.

He dried his hands on the dishtowel and nodded at the clock.

"Mr. Harris says nine, nine-thirty."

"Will I be done with the hallways by then?" I asked.

"That's up to you, Petey," he said. "If you start by seven you should be OK."

After my last sip of coffee, he reached for my cup to wash it.

"But don't rush the job in order to watch them pour the sidewalk," he said. "And don't bother the men while they're working."

Another kiss on my cheek, and my father said, "And when you're finished, Petey, when the floors are dry, roll the bucket to the back of the third floor, and return the mop to the closet. And be sure to look over your work to see that it's tip-top." He put his finger on my cheek and turned my face toward his. "And remember this while you're on the job," he said. "You're a Bellapani." He locked his eyes into mine. "Same as me."

He left for the bakery, then, and I dressed quietly so I wouldn't wake my mother. Minutes later I was in the hallway, sweeping the halls back to front, and the stairs top to bottom, thinking about the cement the whole time. The old sidewalk—before they'd torn it up—had buckled, and through the cracks that cut across it like branches, thorny weeds had begun to grow, but in a couple of hours they'd be pouring cement in front of my eyes, and by tonight there'd be a new sidewalk, smooth and new and almost white.

I walked up to the third floor to soak the mop into the bucket, and dragged it the length of the hallway. The thick mass of mop strings tracked a shiny path along the old brown paint of the floor. I started to mop like they did in the movies, stroking the mop forward and pulling it back, and I could see what my father meant about pushing the dirt around; I could feel the dry film of dust beneath the mop strings, and in the light of the bare light bulb swinging from the ceiling on a ropy cord; I could see the particles of dust swirling at the top of the puddle I pushed along the floor. I tried it side to side, then, walking backward as I mopped, and I thought of my father dancing in the kitchen, swaying with an invisible mop in his hands. I imagined him, when he returned from his deliveries that afternoon, walking through the halls with his hands clasped behind his back, inspecting my work and nodding his head.

After finishing the third floor hallway, I dunked the mop again, and walked to the second floor, the mop dripping wildly on the stairs. An errant string hung lower than the rest of the mop, dragging a thin line to the back of the second floor hallway. As I passed the doors of the second floor apartments, my heartbeat quickened at the possibility of one of them opening up to Gus Valenti. Fucking punk.

I climbed the stairs to rinse the mop out and squeeze it dry in the wringer, and on my way back down, I wiped the stairs where the mop had dripped. After the twice-over on the second floor, the mop was still wet, so instead of rinsing it again, I just wiped it over the stairs to the first floor landing, figuring I'd check my work after it dried. When I leaned the mop behind the open door at the landing, the loose mop string was gone.

Downstairs, the cement guys hadn't started working on the sidewalk yet. Across the street, Joe Harris pointed a long brush at the six and a short one between eight and nine. A ramp had been set over the cementless and shallow pit that had once been a sidewalk, and it bounced with my weight as I reached the middle. Another ramp, at the corner, led to the entrance of the bakery. I exaggerated the bounce as I walked to the glass door, and when I opened it, a whoosh of bakery air swirled around me. Inside the smell was bread and rising dough and sugar, the scent of flour spilled on damp wood, there was cinnamon and yeast, strawberry and lemon. Maria, wearing a baker's hat, and a white apron pulled tight across her chest, transferred coffee cakes from a tall, wheeled rack into the glass counter.

"Petey Bellapani!" She didn't say my name as much as sing it, while she waved at me to join her behind the counter. "Come here with those big brown eyes," she said, and she also said, "Oh my God, I could eat you." Instead of eating me, though, she wiped her hands on her apron and slapped her fat, soft hands against my cheeks. Picking a doughnut from a rack—a custard éclair sprinkled with powdered sugar—she set it on the counter, opened a refrigerator, and pulled a half-pint of chocolate milk from the top shelf and thudded it next to my doughnut. She slapped the seat of a stool next to the cash register, and a voice yelled from the kitchen when I sat down.

"Who is that out there, Maria? Is that Petey Goodbread?" he yelled. It was Mr. Augle, the baker, and that's what he called me: Petey Goodbread.

Maria said, "Take a number, Ralph. It's my turn with Petey, and he's eating, so leave us alone."

"Ah, shuddup," he said, and even though I knew he was kidding, I flinched at the sound of it. Maria smiled at me, though, and she made a fist and clenched it toward the kitchen.

"Make sure you come on back here when she's finished talking your ear off, Goodbread." Mr. Augle called out.

I ate my éclair, and Maria showed me off to the customers who came in. "That's Petey Bellapani sitting behind the counter, there," she'd say. "He's Joe Bellapani's kid." "Best-looking kid in Bridgeport," she'd say, or "Take a look at the eyelashes on that kid." And when another woman came in, she leaned toward her and said, "Spitting image of his father when he was a kid."

When I finished eating, I thanked Maria, and while she hugged me I shut my eyes hard because one of her breasts pressed against my left shoulder and the other against my right. Then I got up and walked toward the kitchen. It was dark there, everything a shade of gray, and I stopped to adjust to the darkness. I couldn't see Mr. Augle, but there was whistling, and when I took a step forward he sprang from behind a rack of empty trays.

"Petey Goodbread!" he shouted, like he hadn't seen me for years.

"Hi, Mr. Augle," I said.

"How's the new apartment, Petey?"

"OK," I said. "We've got a new floor in the kitchen."

The baker held a cannoli shell in one hand and a canvas pastry bag in the other.

"So I heard," he said. "You just missed your old man, by

the way. He picked up a load of doughnuts about two minutes ago. And what did I tell you about that *Mister Augle* crap?" he continued. "I don't care what your old man says. You call me *Ralph* or I'll start charging you for doughnuts."

Hearing him call my father my *old man* made me feel like I'd done something wrong. He pointed the cannoli shell at me like a gun.

"You're lucky this thing ain't loaded," he said, and he put it to his eye as if it were a telescope. "Hey, Petey," he said. "You give me a hand with this batch of cannolis and I'll wiggle my ears for you."

Mr. Augle had bigger ears than any living man, and when he wiggled them, they were like little feet flapping on the sides of his head. It made you forget what you were doing. And he could whistle like a bird.

I held a cannoli shell while he filled one side, and then I flipped it over so he could fill it from the other. He dipped the ends of it into an aluminum bowl of chopped pistachio nuts, and sprinkled it with powdered sugar. He handed me the pastry bag, and as I made some on my own, we talked about school and sports.

He asked me why I wasn't watching cartoons on a Saturday morning, so I told him about my job sweeping and mopping for Mr. Harris.

"Saturday morning, and you're mopping floors!?" He said it so loudly I flinched, and looked around to see if my father was in the bakery.

"You should be watching cartoons, Petey," he continued. "That's what you should be doing! Watching cartoons." He shook his head. "I'm gonna have to sit your old man down and have a talk with him about this," he said, and I hoped he was kidding.

In the time it took me to fill one cannoli, Mr. Augle finished three. Sometimes it was quiet while we worked, but never for too long; he'd start whistling a new song, or singing, or if he felt me looking at him out of the corner of his eye, he'd wiggle his ears and pretend he didn't know I was watching. Another time when it was quiet he brought up the hallway job from out of the blue.

"How old are you now, Petey?"

"Eight."

"Eight years old," he said, and he shook his head at my age. "Mopping floors," he said again. Like it was spit.

"You shouldn't be working at all." He pointed another cannoli at me. "Maybe that's why your old man never smiles, Goodbread. He works too much."

I looked at him to see if he was wiggling his ears, or smiling, but he wasn't; he was only shaking his head. When he picked up the powdered sugar to sprinkle another cannoli, though, he saw me looking at him, and he finally smiled.

"You got a name like Goodbread," he said. "If anything, you should be working in a bakery. That's what you should be doing!" and he started whistling again.

I told him about the cement guys coming to fix the sidewalk, and he acted like he knew nothing about it. "Oh, is that what they're doing out there?" he said. "I wondered who took the sidewalk this morning." He turned toward the store of the bakery and yelled.

"Maria!"

"Whaddya want, Ralph?" she yelled. "I'm trying to run a bakery out here."

Mr. Augle looked at me and rolled his eyes in his head. "She's trying to run a bakery," he said. He yelled back to the storefront. "Make sure you let us know when the cement truck arrives," he said.

"Yeah, yeah, yeah," Maria said.

Mr. Augle left me to the cannolis while he whistled his way around the kitchen, swirling from table to table, pounding dough and twisting it into braided wreaths. He rolled a rack of yellow cake layers to the icing table across from me, spreading out a dozen cardboard discs. He set out a giant aluminum bowl of frosting, a container of rubber spatulas, and three pastry bags tipped with silver nozzles. I filled cannoli shells and watched him ice the cakes.

"You know, Petey," he said. "Maybe I'll come and work for you when you're a baker one day."

We didn't talk much after that. Mr. Augle picked up a silver-tipped pastry bag, and began squeezing strings of white beads in a loopy necklace on the walls of the cake. From the second bag he popped tiny pink hearts, and from the third came flowers—cotton-candy blue. His hands were fast and rhythmic and worked to the song of his whistling. His lips were almost white as he whistled, and pink again when he rested them. When he moistened them between songs, they glistened. His cheeks puffed and pulsed as they gave breath to the sounds, and his lips turned his breathing into music.

When I finished my last cannoli, I wrapped each of them in bakery paper and stacked them into white boxes, and as I closed the last of the boxes, I told Mr. Augle I was done.

"Of course I'll have to inspect your work, Goodbread," he said, and opened one of the boxes to unwrap a cannoli. He looked at each end, and gently flicked a fingernail against the middle of the shell. "Checking for hollow spots," he said. He tested its weight, and brought it to his nose and sniffed, then he put it to the side of his head and shushed me so he could listen to the cannoli. Then he wiggled his ears as if that's what ears did when they paid perfect attention. "Not bad, Petey Goodbread," he said. "Not bad."

Mr. Augle walked toward the storefront as he re-wrapped the cannoli, and when he returned he had a small white bag in his hands. He snapped it open and put the cannoli inside.

"After lunch," he said, and he lifted the bag with the cannoli in it.

Then Maria's voice came from the store of the bakery. "Hey, Petey!" she said. "They're here."

I hopped off the stool and grabbed my cannoli. "Bye, Mr. Augle," I said.

"What did you call me?"

"Sorry."

"Hang on, Petey," he said. He walked me to the storefront and pushed two buttons on the register. A bell rang, and when the cash drawer knocked into his apron, he jumped back and clutched his stomach as though he'd been sucker-punched.

When he recovered, he said, "Hold out your hand, Petey." He pulled a roll of nickels from the register and opened the folds of paper at one end. He tapped three nickels into my hand.

I looked at the nickels and then at him. "I better not take this, Mr. Augle," I said.

"Nonsense," he said. "You earned it. Not only that, but if you make sure nobody steps in the wet cement, I'll give you the rest of the roll later." Winking at me, he continued, "I'm gonna sneak out the side door this afternoon, but I have to pop back after dinner. If you're still out there when I come back, we'll be the first two guys in the neighborhood to pitch nickels on the new sidewalk. I'll teach you how to pitch like a pro." He squinted like he was aiming for the lines, and faked pitching nickels. "I can toss 'em in the groove every time, Petey." He winked at me again. "Oh," he said, "and not a word to your old man about the nickels, Goodbread."

"Thanks, Mr. Ralph," I said.

Outside, a pickup truck pulled to the curb, and two men climbed from its cab. I ran up the stairs to put the cannoli in the refrigerator, and left a note for my mother, who was still sleeping. By the time I returned, two more men had appeared, and the blue cement truck was parked in front of our entrance. It made a shadow like an elephant.

The driver of the cement truck had a cigarette balanced on his ear like a pencil. There was an oval patch on his shirt pocket that said *Bernie*. He pulled a pack of True cigarettes from his pocket, and, looking at the sidewalk framed in two-by-eights, he put a cigarette to his lips. He struck a blue-tipped stick match across the bricks of the bakery and lit his cigarette with the flame while it sizzled.

"How you doin'?" he said to me.

I told him I was fine.

Bernie kept the cigarette in his lips while he worked, the ashes floating from the tip like pieces of a feather.

The truck churned, spilling gray cement down the trunk of the blue elephant. It piled into a mound at the landing, and when the mound tumbled over itself and began spreading like lava, Bernie shifted the chute to start a new hill of cement. The other men grabbed steel-toothed rakes and spread the cement to the edges of the wooden frame.

When the space in front of the doorway was nearly filled with cement, Bernie was standing in front of me blowing cigarette smoke through his nose. The cartoon clock of Joe Harris read nine-thirty. That's when Bernie whistled. He kept his cigarette at the corner of his mouth, folded his lips over his teeth, rolled his tongue, and forced a screaming whistle through the slit of his mouth. It was shrill and piercing, a woman's scream, and the force of it knocked the cigarette from his lips. Bernie twitched as if he'd thought to catch it, but he checked himself, and the cigarette hissed into the muddy mix.

I was close enough to see inside the hollow tip of the rust-colored filter. It was like a peace sign. Bernie didn't bend down to pick it up, like I thought he would, so I reached out from the doorstep to get it. With my fingers an inch away, Bernie stepped on the cigarette with the toe of his rubber boot, burying it in the wet cement like he was crushing a bug.

"Don't sweat it, kid," he said. "Nobody's ever gonna know about it."

Staring at the cement, I was certain there were cigarette butts buried everywhere in the city. I thought of the weeds that grew from the cracks of the old cement, too, and I imagined them waiting there for a crack to appear. I imagined a world of unwanted things—sandwich wrappers, soda cans, chicken bones, and bottle caps—living just beneath the sidewalks of Bridgeport. If Bernie would have left right then, I would have dug into the wet cement with my bare hands to get it, but when I looked up, he was staring right at me, and so I looked away. I was afraid if he looked me in the eye he'd know what I was thinking: that he was a fucking punk.

The men continued to level the mounds from inside the frame until their steps slugged with the setting cement, and then they stepped into the street and began working it smooth from there. Then, with tiny sawing motions, they worked a long two-by-six so tenderly across the cement, you could hardly see them move. Water lifted to the surface and the wet cement slowly became a sidewalk.

They turned on the fire hydrant across the street, rinsed their tools and boots, and ate lunch. Bernie inspected the sidewalk when they finished, and when he said, "Groovin' time," they made measurements with a string and pounded nails in the curbside frame where the groove lines would start. I remembered my three nickels. I stood up and slipped my hand into my pocket for them. All three read "1970." They were so new they were sharp at the edges, and I held them while the men set the grooves.

My mother called from the top of the staircase just before noon, to see if I was hungry, but I wasn't.

"Just let me know when you're hungry," she said.

After setting the grooves, the men placed sawhorses on the old cement that butted against each end of the new sidewalk, returned the ramps, one to my stairwell and the other to the bakery door, packed their tools, and pulled away. Across the street, Joe Harris's hands pointed at the twelve.

I patrolled the curb from ramp to ramp with my hands behind my back. The sun shone directly above me. When people passed by, I stood to let them know I was in charge of the sidewalk, and that the cement was still wet. If they were going to the bakery, I pointed to the ramp at the corner.

My father returned from his last delivery at one-fifteen. His eyes were tired.

"Nice sidewalk," he said, and, without waiting for my response, added, "How'd it go this morning?"

I thought he was talking about the cement. "OK, so far," I said.

"Let's inspect the halls," he said.

"Could we do it later, Dad? Mr. Augle asked me to guard the cement."

He nodded. "I'll take a look at them after my nap."

I wanted him to smile, but he didn't.

"Did you eat yet?" he asked.

"I've been working," I said.

"That's my boy," he said. "I'll have mom make a grilled cheese sandwich for you."

As he walked up the stairs, I wanted to call after him, *Wait*, but I didn't. I had left the mop behind the door at the landing, and if he looked back he would have seen it. I wondered if he'd notice the stairs I'd only gone over once, or if he'd notice a film of dust where I'd mopped up and back like in the movies, and the sound of him swearing came back to me.

Minutes later, I heard my mother's careful steps coming down the long flight of stairs. She'd quartered the grilled cheese sandwich, and between each piece, had sprinkled potato chips. Unwrapping the cannoli, she sat next to me, and clinked a glass of lemonade between us. I asked her if she'd seen the hallways.

"They look great," she said.

"Did you look closely?" I asked. "Dad told me to make sure I checked them, but I didn't."

"Don't worry about it, Petey," she said.

"And I left the bucket at the top of the stairs."

"Don't worry, Petey," she said.

"I don't want him to be mad at me," I said.

She opened her eyes wide and pressed her teeth together. "You did a great job, Petey," she said. "I told Dad it was your first day with a real job."

The bell over Joe Harris's door tinkled. An old woman passing the store shaded her eyes and looked through the window. I thought about how I'd worked for Mr. Harris in the morning, and I was working for him now, too, since he owned the building. And I was also working for Mr. Augle, and for the city in a way, because of all the people who used this sidewalk.

I was working for my father, too, and everyone who would ever walk on this cement for years to come. The sun crept behind Dressel's Bakery.

At three o'clock, my mother brought me a root beer Popsicle, and told me the hallways looked fine, but I wondered how closely she'd checked them.

By 3:30, the concrete looked hard enough to walk on. I swept my finger across a small section. It felt hard and cool and damp, like a shadow. I knelt at the curbside and pressed my thumb to a spot, and it left no mark there, either. I set my Popsicle stick down where the street met the curb and took a nickel from my pocket, placing it in the closest groove. I pretended I'd pitched it there. Everyone would want to pitch nickels here, I thought, and the shadow of the bakery slowly crossed the street.

It was nearly dinnertime when I saw him walking toward me from Thirty-second Street. Brown hair, dago-tee, cigarette dangling from his lips. Gus Valenti. My heart beat like a fist against my chest. I looked at the stairs behind me. Thirty-three steps to my father.

Until then, I'd protected the sidewalk by standing up when people passed, but they were all grown-ups. Gus was fifteen, a teenager, and he'd made my father swear. I pressed my thumb against the cement again. It felt hard. I pressed the heel of my hand against it. I stretched my right foot past the bottom step, and touched the toe of my shoe to the concrete. Nothing. But was it solid enough to hold the weight of a punk?

Gus had reached the Romanos' garden when he put his cigarette to his lips for a final drag, his fingers and thumb in the shape of OK. He pulled deep and long and gave it one last look before flicking it just past the middle of the street. I wondered if a punk would have flicked a cigarette differently. Maybe a punk would've flicked it right onto the new cement, or maybe he would have stamped it out right into the cement, or even flicked it in my face. Still, I wanted him to be up the stairs over my shoulder, opening his apartment door. I wanted him to be far away.

Gus stopped at the bottom of the ramp and stared at the

twelve squares of fresh cement folding around the corner of Dressel's Bakery. He backed up, glancing at the windows of our apartment, then looked at the perfect curb of cement before him, still framed in wood. He did a double take to his right, his eyes locked on something in the street. I couldn't tell what it was until he picked it up and wiped it on his jeans. My Popsicle stick. He knelt at the first square of new cement and began to scratch at it with the Popsicle stick. He started with a straight line, going over it several times, the thin wood of the Popsicle stick scratching until it made a sharp-edged scar in the surface.

I wanted Mr. Augle to come by in his car right then, or Joe Harris to open the door of the hardware store and come across the street to help me. I wanted to scream or rush upstairs to get my father, or run down the ramp to stop Gus from ruining the cement, but I didn't do anything. I just sat there with my heart hammering against my chest.

Gus looked up at me after he made the straight line, and then blocked what he was writing with his arm as if he were protecting it from a cheater. A piece of the stick broke off, and he poked the rest of his message into the sidewalk, forcing the Popsicle stick into the setting cement. There were no cars on Wallace Avenue, there was only the sound of wood scraping into cement.

Then Gus stood up, stepped back, and wiped his hands on his blue jeans. From where I sat, the words were upside down, but it looked like there were numbers. I wondered if he'd written the date so that in a hundred years people would know when the cement had been poured. But it didn't matter anyway, he'd ruined the sidewalk. He nodded and dropped what was left of the stick into the street, and stepped toward me, bouncing as he approached the middle of the ramp.

He stopped in front of me, and I was afraid to face him.

"What's your name, kid?"

I looked up, tried to answer, but my throat stuck.

"Petey Bellapani," I finally said.

"See you later, Petey Bee." He mussed my hair and sprang up the stairs.

I didn't move. Even when the door to his apartment opened and shut behind me, I just sat there. My pulse beat against my temples. I wondered if my father hated Gus Valenti enough to move to another neighborhood, or even another city. I thought it would be OK if we moved. I watched the shadow of the bakery move across Gus's message and into the street. When I finally stood, my bones stiff, I walked across the ramp to the curb, where I read the words he'd written.

*Fuck you Mary Nelson 1970.*

I knelt down and traced the words with my finger. I stepped on the f-word with all my weight, and twisted the toe of my shoe into it. I scuffed at it with my heel. I picked up what was left of the Popsicle stick and scraped at it, but it was too late. My father would wake from his nap, soon, and see the words Gus had written.

I thought of the nickels, then, and checked to see if they were still in my pocket. The rest of the roll was in the cash register in the bakery. It would stay there, and I'd return these nickels to Mr. Augle, too. My job was to guard the cement, but I didn't do it. I couldn't stop a punk from swearing in the cement.

Gus Valenti was a fucking punk. Even though he called me "Petey Bee" and mussed my hair like a grown-up, Gus Valenti was a fucking punk. My father was right about that. My father was smart.

I tried to erase the words from my thoughts, but there was nothing else to replace them. *Fuck you Mary Nelson* was all there was to think.

I climbed halfway up the stairs and then back down to see if I would notice the words when I left the apartment each day. There they were. They were upside down, but there they were, like a little kid's handwriting.

When Mr. Augle pulled up in his yellow station wagon with wood paneling on the side, I was still on my doorstep. The sun had set a million miles behind the bakery. Mr. Augle walked around the front of the car, smiling, and was just about to say my name when he stopped at the curb. Then he looked into my eyes and down at the cement. He stared at the words Gus had written. He shook his head slowly and wiped his shoe across the words.

When he finally looked up at me in the doorway of my stairwell, I wanted to tell him everything, how I'd watched the men work, and how Bernie had dropped his cigarette in the wet cement and how I'd wanted to uncover it. I wanted to tell him I had worked all day, had swept and mopped the hallways in the building, and filled cannolis in the bakery, but I couldn't stop Gus Valenti, and I didn't even try to stop him, and I wanted to ask him if he knew who Mary Nelson was, because I wanted to apologize to her, but I was afraid I'd start to cry if I said anything.

My name is Bellapani, I was thinking. It was still Petey Bellapani.

And then Mr. Augle walked up the ramp, and sat next to me. I could see flour in his fingernails, and smell the bakery on his clothes and in his hair. We were looking at the words in the cement, and he put his arm on my shoulder.

"My father," I said, and I started to cry.

And all Mr. Augle said was, "Shhh, shhh. Don't you worry about your father, Petey. I'll talk to him."

"Please don't be mad at him, Mr. Augle," I said, and I shut my teeth hard trying not to cry again, but it came out in a burst that puffed my cheeks and exploded from my mouth.

"Shhh," he said again, and when I caught my breath and stopped crying he spoke again. "Nobody's mad at your father, Petey," he said. The tiniest dusting of flour stuck to the hairs on his arms. "Your father's a good man."

After a while Mr. Augle stepped off the bottom stair onto the new cement as if testing the coolness of water. Confidently, he lifted the ramp from the middle and set it on the Romano's sidewalk next door.

"Don't go anywhere, Goodbread," he said. "I'll be right back."

He bounced up the other ramp to the bakery, and fumbling through his keys he opened the bakery door, and disappeared. A square of light reflected on the new cement. When he came out again, he walked down the ramp, balancing his arms at his side, like it was a tight rope, and then he tested the cement again, his footing deliberate and irregular. When he was certain it was solid, he tap-danced a few steps.

"Do you still have those nickels, Petey?"

I dug in my pocket, and when I handed him the nickels, he shook them like dice.

"Let's see now," he said. He stood with his toes against a groove in the cement, squinting at a line two squares away, and tossed the first coin. It clinked and bounced two inches from the target groove. "Ouch," he grunted. Hunching down, he tossed again, this time exaggerating his follow-through, holding his hand out long after the toss, and clenching his teeth as the nickel floated through a high arc. It hit the ground and bounced onto the groove, a shiny bridge between the two squares of cement.

"That's more like it," he said, and he tossed the third coin, which followed the exact arc of the coin before, and bounced and rolled neatly into the groove. Then he walked toward me and reached into his pocket. He pulled out the roll of nickels, clapped it across my palm, and closed my fingers around it.

A roll of nickels is heavy. In the shell of my hand, the ends of the roll poked out the sides. Mr. Augle sat next to me, holding an imaginary nickel in his right hand as if he were getting ready to toss it. Elbows on his knees, he bounced the invisible nickel in preparation for an imaginary toss.

"The thing about pitching nickels, Petey Goodbread," he said, "is this..."

# Blessed the Fruit

**W**hen I woke for my paper route on Saturday morning it was 5:00 A.M. The note my father had left for me said this:

> *Should be fine today.*
> *Raincoat, just in case. Wrap*
> *the papers in plastic bags.*
> *Wet from last night. Wake*
> *me up when you get back.*

He'd written the note after the weather report on the ten o'clock news, and had fallen to an easy sleep on his faith in the weatherman and the chance of rain.

There were things to fight against in Bridgeport, but nature wasn't one of them. There were no angry seas, no wind-swept plains. It was cold in the winter, wet in the spring, hot in the summer, and in the autumn it was all of these. But while we slept through that Friday night in June, a thunderstorm raged through the neighborhood. Thunder exploded and ropes of lightning rent the sky. Under the roofs of two-flats and storefronts, children climbed into

beds with parents. Alley cats crouched under porches, screen
doors slammed, windows rattled and banged, and the wind
flung forgotten porch chairs against doors. The city became
another place—a farm in Nebraska or Kansas or some other
place where violent weather was no surprise—where a smell, a
color of sky, or the whimper of a dog announced such events.
No one saw it coming in Bridgeport, though. No one could
smell a storm before it clocked him in the eye.

Outside, it was so dark I thought I'd made a mistake and
woke up too early. The clock above Joe Harris Hardware said
eleven twenty-two, which wasn't much help. It had stopped the
night before. There was no moon, and the street lamps were
out. No light came from the bakery windows.

On my way through the gangway to get to my wagon from
under the back porch, I wished I had a flashlight. The gangway
was a tunnel of darkness, a cave. A grapevine arbor spilled over
from the Romanos' yard next door, and I brushed my fingers
along it to guide myself through the tunnel.

In the darkness my fingers bumped against a bunch of
grapes that poked through the chain-link fence, and I stopped
to pluck one. The skin of it was rubbery and thick, and it peeled
away from the inside like sunburned skin. Inside, the pulp was
phlegmy and cool like the meat of an aloe plant and the color,
as well, though it was too dark out to see. I felt the zing of the
bitter juice in my jaw before I even put it in my mouth. It was
bitter and seedy and I chewed it hard and fast, and swallowed
the juice—it always surprised me, how much there was—and
then I spit it out like I always did, and shook my head at the
phlegmy bitterness. It was hard to believe that wine could ever
come from grapes, but a full wooden barrel in the Romanos'
house was proof that it did.

The grapevine was a blunt-edged horseshoe around the
front and sides of the garden. It opened up at the tiny brick
house that backed against the alley like a garage. There was a
row of fig trees that lined the patio at the front of the house, too,
and within the shoe formed by the grapevines and the figs was

a miracle of a garden. Even through the smell of bread that had baked itself forever into the bricks of my building, you could smell the Romanos' garden, the grapes and everything.

Even the dirt was a miracle. Everywhere else in Bridgeport, dirt was dry and gray, it was dusty and smelled like nothing. It was dirty. But in the Romanos' garden the dirt was black and rich and soft and smelled like the perfect union of all the things that came from it, as if you put two of everything—the grapes, peppers, tomatoes, swiss chard, and everything else—in a big brown paper bag, that's what the dirt smelled like. It was more like food than dirt. It was loamy and dark and things grew from it.

The garden was the greenest, most living thing in all of Bridgeport. There was parsley, swiss chard, and radishes, turnips, potatoes, green and red bell peppers, Serrano peppers, pepperoncini, beefsteak, cherry and plum tomatoes, and a broccoli patch that grew so thick in midsummer you could hide in it. There were carrots, basil, mint, and lettuce. And reeds of garlic, wild and disobedient, grew wherever they wanted.

And rising from an unbricked square of dirt in the heart of the patio was a cherry tree. Its roots flexed like ancient muscles, holding fast, it seemed, to some solid thing a mile inside the earth, like talons. The bricks of the patio buckled around the trunk, which was thick and black and grew into something rich and green, dotted with red—a child's drawing—and it stood above the tiny house like a soldier.

Mr. Romano had planted the tree thirty years before. He'd chosen the space for it, had removed bricks from the patio and had knelt to plant the seed, and still I wondered at the geography of it. The Romanos had come from Italy to Bridgeport. Of all the states and all the cities and all the neighborhoods in America. They might have gone to Florida or Georgia or a place that was warm in February, or where there were already cherry trees, but they'd come here, to plant one in the middle of a place where fruit had never grown. That was something. You could plant the seed of a cherry in a place like this and one day there'd be a cherry tree in the place of the planting. And Mr. Romano cared for it like a child. He watered it, fed the dirt around it. He'd made something like crutches when the tree couldn't bear its own young weight. He trimmed it as it grew, he spoke to it, he built a garden and a life around it, and a month before it bore a single cherry, he sat against the base of it, folded his hands over his chest, and took a nap from which he never woke up.

I wondered at all of it, not just the tree. I had even seen a rabbit in the Romanos' garden once, in the middle of nowhere. The garden was like a mistake in the city. It was like a farm. Families from the other side of the viaduct took walks on summer nights and the Romanos' garden was their destination. They'd stop at the sidewalk and just stand there staring, as if it were a horse clopping by in a horseless place.

And behind it all, behind the garden and the grapevines and the fig trees and the cherry tree and the buckled brick patio, their house was a toy, like something made for children, a clubhouse or treehouse, and you felt like ducking when you went inside.

But in the darkness that Saturday morning in June, I couldn't see any of it. I pulled my wagon from under the porch behind the bakery, and wheeled back through the gangway and up the cement steps to the street.

On the corner of Thirty-first Street, behind the glass wall of the Wallace News office, bright bulbs of light flared into the darkness. Up close, the light bulbs swung from ropy cords, bare and shocking, like skulls.

I opened the door and set free a dry haze of newspaper fumes. It was like coming into a coal mine, and a sooty veil curled around me and snuck into my nose like fingers. It was thick and inky and smelled like gray dirt and green rubber bands. Inside the office, the walls bore the faded legacy of lime-green paint, left over from the days when my father had delivered papers from the same office. Bundles of newspapers struggled against plastic bands in stacks piled high against the walls. Above the stacks, the blackened handprints of generations of boys were stamped and smeared on every wall.

I counted out twenty-seven *Sun-Timeses*, and nineteen *Tribunes*, and carried them to the table against the south wall. I rolled and rubber-banded the *Sun-Times* newspapers and wrapped them in plastic bags. President Nixon was on the cover, and every time I rolled one up and wrapped it in plastic, there he was again on the pile in front of me. He was on the front page of the *Tribune*, too. *Tribunes* were thicker, though–you had to fold them in half to fit them in the plastic bags. I loaded the newspapers onto my wagon, and covered them with a sheet of blue tarpaulin. I secured the bundles with rubber cords, and when I opened the door, my hands were black with ink. The air outside was damp. Fresh.

I made the sign of the cross, and prayed for people in the places that always made the headlines. I prayed for people in Belfast and Turkey and China and France. I prayed for President Nixon and the soldiers in Vietnam, and for the U.S. table-tennis team. And then I prayed for people I knew from St. David's. There was Johnny Foglio, who was nine—same as me—but his mother had already died. I always prayed for him. And there was Christine Lunning, who was poorer than even we were. I prayed for a girl that everyone called Dirty Joanne, too. And Timmy Bokina. He only went to school with us for the last month of fourth grade, but I prayed for him. He came to the Wallace Playlot one day and gave all of us a dollar—me and Chucky and Matty and Ronny and Davy. We all bought bottles of pop. I bought an RC Cola and a small bag of Swedish Fish, and I don't remember why, but it was the saddest day. My paper route was one long prayer.

But then I'd walk up someone's stairs—like Mr. Russo's or someone—to deliver a paper and I'd see inside their window and I would forget about the prayer. Or I would start *thinking* about those people—like Johnny Foglio or Timmy Bokina or whoever—instead of praying for them. I'd wonder what it was like for Johnny to go home and not have his mother there anymore. Or I'd wonder where Timmy Bokina was going to school or where he got that money from. Or I'd think about playing softball, or how the new cement by the Zakiches' house was so smooth, or how in the Considines' hallway it always smelled like dessert. And then something would happen, or nothing would happen at all, and I'd remember the prayer. I would remember that I was inside the signs of the cross that opened and closed prayer, and until I made the sign of the cross that ended it, everything that happened was a kind of praying. I knew even then that it was okay if I forgot about prayer while praying. I used to think that God didn't mind when I forgot.

Walking west on Thirty-first Street toward Emerald Avenue where my paper route was, I looked at the sun rising behind me, remembering how dark it had been when I first left the bakery building. You couldn't see Lake Michigan from there, but I imagined the sun rising over the lake. It was like a flashlight struggling through a sheet of clouds. When I turned back around, there was a steel dumpster standing upright in the middle of the street. It was painted red and had *Bridgeport Foods* stenciled on its side. Then I noticed all the garbage in the street. Between Wallace and Lowe, fifty-five gallon garbage drums lay tipped on their sides, their contents dumped and scattered through the alley. There was litter everywhere. I rolled my wagon around a paper plate stained with spaghetti sauce. In the street and on the sidewalk, everywhere I looked, there was garbage: tin cans, rags, paper grocery bags soaked and torn; there were cereal boxes, fruit rinds, egg shells, and lifeless drooping cardboard boxes—everything soiled and stained with the scrapings from a thousand kitchen plates, the soupy drippings from the bottoms of kitchen trash bags.

Less than a mile away, on the funneled entrance to the viaduct on Twenty-sixth and Canal, there was a mural, a painted skyline of Bridgeport, behind hosed-down sidewalks and working-class lawns. And through the painted neighborhood, rising high above the rooftops, swelled the proud, glowing spires and belfries of a dozen churches. Spreading like a rainbow of letters over the mural, a caption read, "Bridgeport, Neighborhood of Churches." But the still-sleeping neighborhood of churches would awaken in an hour or so to the stinking and rotten truth that it was a neighborhood of alleys as well, and alleys were where we kept our garbage. And overnight, it had been tumbled and blown by a heartless and indiscriminate storm, the detritus of us discovered to the world.

The garbage wasn't so bad past Lowe Avenue where there was a children's park, made of cement and iron, on one side of Thirty-first Street, and St. John's Lutheran Church on the other. When I crossed the light at Union Avenue, I said a prayer for Mrs. Pell. She was the crossing guard and that was her corner. She told me to walk between the lines one day and I didn't know what she meant, so I walked on one of the white lines like it was a tightrope painted on the ground. It seemed like such a crazy thing to want me to do, and she gave me a look like I was being a smart aleck. She pulled my mother aside when she saw us at church the next Sunday, and told her about what I did.

There wasn't much garbage on Emerald Avenue, either, where I turned to begin delivering my newspapers. But there were trees on Emerald, and a storm that could push dumpsters around like toy trucks can play with trees, too. Leaves and branches were scattered everywhere. On Thirtieth and Emerald, in front of the Steggmillers' house, the great limb of a maple tree blocked the sidewalk. At its broken end, the wood was pale yellow, with a streak of black through the middle. While I walked across the street to roll my wagon around the end of the limb, a car wheeled slowly up to the felled tree, but there was no way around it, and the driver backed up the car and turned around at the end of the street.

I stopped when I reached the tree in front of Mr. and Mrs. Solis's house. There were only a few leaves sprinkled at its base, otherwise there was nothing wrong with it. I wondered how some trees had escaped damage, and wondered also if trees had feelings, wondered if they were sorry they couldn't help the other trees as their branches were ripped away. I thought about Mr. Romano then. All the stories my father had told me about him, and all I could see was him lying at the base of the tree in the deepest of sleeps.

I remembered about the prayer then. I said a prayer for Mr. and Mrs. Romano, and when I delivered a *Tribune* to Mr. and Mrs. Solis's house, I said one for them, too. They both smoked cigarettes, and they coughed in a way that hurt my chest just to hear it. I said one for Stevie Solis, too. He wrote his name backwards on a Mother's day card one day, and after that everyone called him Nevets. And I prayed for my parents, and Chucky and those guys, and some other kids from St. David's, like Paully Pavisek, who didn't have any sweat glands. I prayed for Mayor Daley, too, and Joe Harris, and the driver of the car that had to turn around because of the tree.

When I got to Twenty-ninth, I crossed the street and headed back south to deliver papers on the west side of Emerald. Ten or so houses down the block, the limb of another tree had broken through the windshield of a green Matador, and what I wanted to do was fix everything. I wanted to return every limb of every tree to the oak or maple to which it belonged, and to roll every garbage can back to the address painted on its side, and sweep through every street with a push broom and shovel, and hide all the garbage. Restore the neighborhood to the thing it was before the storm. I wanted the people of Bridgeport to awaken to the same world they'd put to sleep a few hours before.

On my way back home, the dumpster was still standing in the middle of Thirty-first Street, and I wheeled my wagon onto Wallace, which seemed to have been spared of litter, except near the mouths of the alleys on either side. At the sidewalk between the bakery and Mrs. Romano's house, I stopped and opened the gate. My hands were dry, and black with ink, and I swung the gate open and started down the stairs. Halfway through the gangway, under the light peeking through the vines on the overhead trellis, I looked into the Romanos' garden, and saw the cherry tree lying crippled on the garden floor, its trunk split three feet from the bottom, crushing broccoli, lettuce, and carrots along the northern trellis of the grapevine. Pale splinters, thick and charred, stood up like stalagmites from the base of the trunk. Its fruit-laden crown lay flattened on the garden floor.

Returning the wagon to my back porch, I looked back at the tree, and wondered where lightning came from, and how far it traveled, and how it made decisions. Did it hit houses, too, or just people and trees?

I climbed the stairs to the bakery apartment and opened our door on the third floor to wake my father for his part-time job; he delivered bread and wedding cakes for the bakery on weekends. I touched his shoulder and whispered.

"Dad."

He moaned, pretending to be fast asleep.

"Dad," I repeated.

He shrugged my hand from his shoulder and grunted, like a kid who didn't want to go to school. But then he smiled.

"Morning, Petey," he said. "What time is it?"

"Six-thirty."

"Thanks, Petey. I'm up," he whispered. "You ought to lay down and get some sleep. How was your paper route?"

"Fine," I said. My mother hadn't moved. "Dad?"

"Yeah?"

"It's Mrs. Romano's cherry tree."

"What about it?"

"I think it was struck by lightning last night."

"What do you mean?" he said.

"I mean it *was* struck by lightning. It's lying on the ground."

He swung his feet over the bed and slid them into his slippers. "Does Mrs. Romano know?"

"I'm not sure," I said. "She wasn't out there."

We walked to the dining room window that overlooked the Romanos' lot. My father swept the curtain to one side and stood there in his T-shirt and boxers. There was a bleach hole the size of a crumb under his left shoulder blade.

"She knows," he said.

I filled the space under his arm, and looked out the window. Mrs. Romano sat in a chair on the patio, staring at the fallen length of the tree, smoothing a dishtowel across her lap.

My father went into his bedroom without a word. When he came out, he was wearing his Saturday work clothes, dark blue pants and a blue collared shirt, and we walked through the long hallway and down the stairs, and then through the gate into Mrs. Romano's garden. My father walked along the path to where she sat, but I sat on the bottom step because I didn't know what to say to her. Mrs. Romano didn't lift her head to greet him. She kept staring at the fallen tree. My father walked behind her and stood there saying nothing for a long time. Then he said something in Italian, and Mrs. Romano nodded her head.

I wondered what he'd said to her, if there were any words he could possibly say that would mean anything after what had happened. There didn't seem to be English words for it. Listening to the sounds he made, though—full and round, soft like music—it seemed as if there might be an Italian way to say the things that should be said in a moment like this. Seconds later, he started toward me.

"Let's go, Petey," he said. "I've got a wedding cake and two restaurant deliveries. We'll come back and check on her when we're done."

We picked up a cake in three separate pieces from Dressel's Bakery, along with two long brown bags of bread and rolls, and set them in the back of the van. I held two of the cake boxes steady across my lap, and held the third on the floor of the car between my feet. My father drove slowly, as though there were a wedding cake on the roof of the van, looking back at me in the rear view mirror every block to check on the cake.

My father was always looking for the lesson in everything. He'd squint as he listened to a song on the radio, concentrating on the lyrics, as if they belonged to a sermon Father Ahern was giving. Sometimes he would turn off the radio and in the quiet that followed a song he'd say, "Did you hear that, Petey? Did you listen to the words?" And then he'd tell me about the point the singer seemed to be making. "Every single one of these songs is about love," he'd say. Sometimes it seemed as though he didn't agree with the song. "Do you think this singer knows about love?" he would say. And sometimes he was in perfect agreement with the singer, or he'd hear a single line of a song like "My Way," and he'd turn off the radio and he'd tell me what was meant by *biting off more than you could chew*. He did it with that line one day.

Or we would watch Fahey Flynn in his bow ties on the nightly news, and during the commercials my father would remark about something that happened during the day, as if he and Fahey Flynn were in cahoots to make some sense of the world.

After we left Mrs. Romano's garden, my father was quiet, though. We delivered the bags of bread to two restaurants, one on Taylor Street, and one on Thirty-fifth and Halsted, and neither of us said a word. Only when we delivered the wedding cake to a banquet hall in Chinatown did my father say anything, and then it was only to talk his way through the construction of the cake.

"You see how Mr. Augle left this inch-or-so band uniced at the bottom of each layer? That's so I can get my fingers in there and set the tiers on right without messing up the icing, you see? Then, after I get all the tiers set right, I look at the cake from above to see that it's properly balanced." He stood on a chair next to the table. "I *eyeball* it to see if it's centered just right."

Satisfied with the look from above, he stepped down from the chair. "When the layers are set just right, I take the pastry bag and decorate these uniced bands with a garland of teardrops or roses or something. Beautiful teardrops, huh? Most people think you have to be some kind of artist to make a cake beautiful like this," he said. "They think it's all about loading the cake up with roses and garlands and leaves and stuff. But you see this here?" He pointed to a section where the icing was plain. "And this here? All blank space. It's the undecorated space that makes a cake beautiful," he said. "Nice, huh?"

He stepped back from the table to look at the cake as if he were a guest at a wedding. It *was* nice, as if Mr. Augle had put it together himself at the icing table in back of Dressel's Bakery.

When we climbed back into the van and began the drive down Wentworth Avenue, my father fell quiet again, but at Twenty-sixth Street he began to speak. This time, it was about Mrs. Romano's garden. He told me how garlic grew and how the seeds of the fig trees had come from Calabria. He talked about the cherry tree. He said that Mrs. Romano had planned to pick the cherries today. He talked about Mr. Romano, too. How he'd loved his wife. How he'd come to Chicago and worked in a peanut-butter factory for years, sending money to his wife, who stayed in Calabria until they saved enough to buy this little house. How he had taken care of the cherry tree and died before it bore fruit. He talked about how carefully Mrs. Romano had tended to it after her husband's death. He also told me how he'd seen Mrs. Romano crying once while she was picking cherries, and how he thought she was probably crying about her husband. I was glad I was in the van to hear these things, because it seemed as though if I wasn't there, he might still have been saying them.

"Mrs. Romano makes her own peanut brittle," he said. "And peanut butter, too. And she makes her own soap."

"She prays the rosary three times each day," he said. "Once for the Sorrowful, once for the Joyful, once for the Glorious Mysteries." And he told me about Italy, a place he had never been, and all the while I was thinking about Mrs. Romano, and Mr. Romano, too, and I wondered what the lesson was in lightning.

After we delivered the final bag of bread to a restaurant on Archer Avenue, we returned the van to the bakery and picked up a small box of Italian cookies for Mrs. Romano.

She was still sitting in her garden, on the same chair, with the dishtowel on her lap. It was decorated with twin cherries, their stems connected like wishbones. We walked through the gate, and I sat on the steps, while my father joined Mrs. Romano at the base of the tree. He set the cookies on the patio without a word and picked up an empty milk crate from against the wall. Turning it over, he brought it next to her and sat down. I watched them as they stared silently at the fallen tree, and slowly the morning unfolded.

It was damp and warm and somber. A small group had gathered on the sidewalk just over my shoulder, a few moms in a whispering assembly. Soon after, the children on our block emerged, sleepily, from their houses. It was mostly younger kids, but my friend Matty Vaccarello was there, too, and his mother was among the group of women. By eleven o'clock the group had grown to ten children, plus Matty and me, and in the energy of each other, the younger ones began whispering about the cherries on the tree. They wondered at what would happen with them.

I considered the miracle of how the storm had come *after* the cherries had ripened, just before they were to be picked.

It was late in the morning when my father rose from his milk crate and stood for a moment beside Mrs. Romano. He smiled down at her and squeezed her shoulder. Then he walked to the sidewalk to speak with the moms assembled at the gate. The circle tightened around him. He gestured toward the tree, and there was a shaking and nodding of heads. Matty and I walked toward my father and the younger children joined us.

"Go to your homes," he told the children. "Mrs. Romano would like you to return with bowls and pots and pans, and fill them with cherries."

Matty looked at me, and smiling, said, "I'll be back in a jiffy, Petey Boy," and he was gone.

While the other children scattered up their stairs and into their cupboards for mixing bowls, my mother walked to where I stood at the Wallace side of the grapevine. She fingercombed my hair off my forehead and scratched my back.

"Are you okay, Petey?" she asked.

And I wasn't sure, but I nodded my head. "Is it all right if I stay here with Dad?" I said.

She combed my hair with her fingers again. "Sure, sweetie," she said.

"But I want cherries, too," I said.

My mother looked at me and smiled. "I'll get a bowl," she said. She touched my father's back, too, before she left. She made apologies to the other moms and began the short walk to our apartment for a mixing bowl.

I stayed with my father at the fence, his hand, pale, almost blue-gray, resting on mine. I pressed on the thick blue vein running down the middle, until he spoke.

"*Guarda*, Petey," he said, and nodded toward Mrs. Romano.

I'd been watching her all along. She walked a slow path around the fallen tree before settling to kneel where its two lowest, thickest limbs stretched out left and right in a vee, like arms. Unfolding the dishtowel, she spread it on the cool earth at her knees. She brushed her fingers over several cherries before settling on one and plucking it from the fallen tree. She placed it on the dishtowel, which she folded around the cherry, and carried the packet to her chair at the trunk of the tree. Sitting down, she unfolded the towel on her lap. She sat there looking at the cherry, unaware or unconcerned that my father and I were watching. Taking it in her right hand, she swung it from the stem gently for a few seconds. Then she removed the stem and rolled the cherry around with her finger before taking it into her mouth. She closed her eyes, and it seemed then that the sun began to burn away the clouds.

Mrs. Romano rolled the cherry whole in her mouth, between her gums and teeth, on her tongue and under it, balancing it gently in the front of her mouth between her teeth. She bit into it, then. I felt her working the cherry in her mouth. I could feel her teeth bite into the middle of the cherry, the meat of the cherry separate from the pit, the pit slip away, half naked, from the bite of her front teeth. I felt her remove the other half of the cherry pulp, and I saw her swallow, and felt her tongue around the pit that remained in her mouth. I could feel the bit of flesh that stuck to the seam of the pit, before she worked it clean.

Behind us, my mother rejoined the others, holding the big,

aluminum mixing bowl on her hip. She was smiling. I turned toward Mrs. Romano again. Her hands were on her lap, and the cherry pit was still in her mouth.

Above us, the clouds floated east, and the brilliant light of the sun washed down the tiny house behind Mrs. Romano, and across the garden and over my father and me. And Mrs. Romano lifted her face—eyes still closed—to the new sun.

Her cheeks shone in the sun, and it was then—when I saw a sparkling trail of the summer sun on her cheeks—that I realized this piece of ground, on the red and brown bricks of the patio, in the garden of the Romanos, in the neighborhood of Bridgeport—was a new place for the sun to shine. For thirty years or more this place had felt nothing but shade; Mr. Romano had died there in a cool blanket of it. And now Mrs. Romano's face was lifted to the sun. Perhaps my father was thinking the same thing. He put his arm across my shoulder.

Her face still raised to the sky, Mrs. Romano lifted the dishtowel from her lap and wiped her eyes. Then she re-spread the towel on her lap. She lifted her hand to her mouth and with the tip of her tongue pushed the cherry pit into the well of her palm, where it blent with the color of her skin. She placed the pit on the dishtowel and folded the edges of the cloth around it, and then she put the cloth into the pocket of her apron and looked up to us at the sidewalk. She nodded to my father.

My father turned around to address the children, vessels in every hand, and said, *"Andiamo, ragazzi."* Let us go, children, and he opened the gate.

I stayed at the fence and watched Mrs. Romano while the rest of the children ran, as if it were recess, through the gate into her garden. She bowed her head and made the sign of the cross, and as she lowered her right hand to her lap, where it joined her left hand in a kind of amen, I wondered if I had closed my prayer at the end of my paper route.

I joined the other children in the garden. The tree seemed much larger now, so laden with cherries that each of us had only to select a space around its great round mass and begin picking.

My bowl was barely half-filled when a flock of shadows flitted over us. I looked up at a hundred birds on their way to the sun. Speechless and smiling—the dirt cool and damp on our knees—we must have been something to see.

# The Wallace Playlot

Somewhere east of Bridgeport, the summer sun rises each day like bread dough, and sixteen hours later, west of St. David's, it settles neatly into the last sidewalk groove in the world like a big yellow nickel. Between these risings and settings, it bakes the Wallace Playlot into cornmeal yellow and plays with the shadows of boys.

Across the street, two floors above the swinging white sign of Dressel's Bakery, my mother calls me home from our living room window. Her voice is soft, trebled, and her lips move in the shape of my name.

"Petey."

Light and carefree, like the beginning of a song, as if it doesn't matter whether I come home or not.

Her second call is more musical. "Peteeeeey. Dinner time," and she holds on to *time* for a few seconds.

When she screams for distance on her third call, it seems her throat wants clearing. It is empty of beauty, this attempt–a creak and screech of a musicless song that reaches me as I stand at home plate with a bat in my hands. Too far away to hear me argue for one more inning, too close to ignore.

"Petey Bella*paneeeeee*. Let's *go-ohhh*."

It was 1972, the last summer of the Wallace Playlot, the summer that started with a punch in the belly from a punk named Hucker Norton, and would end with monstrous machines clawing sores into the earth to make way for new homes. There would be no pickets over the playlot's destruction, no sit-ins or townhalls, no hunger strikes or letters to the editor. A special attention was necessary for that kind of protest, and by virtue of our boyhood we were excused from paying it. We had a canvas bag filled with softballs and bats, and we had the summer: three months of afternoons hanging before us like holidays. Ninety Saturdays in a row. We cared only about the sun and rain, because they were what made our days, or broke them. The future was the next half-inning, and the world outside of Bridgeport was a world away.

What little I did know of the outside world came from my paper route. I delivered twenty-seven *Sun-Timeses* and nineteen *Tribune*s to forty-five houses on Emerald Avenue (Mr. Russo ordered both papers). As I loaded them into my wagon one at a time to keep them stacked and straight, the headlines proclaimed the news of the world: *National Guard Opens Fire, Four Dead; Executed Vietnamese Float Down Mekong; President Nixon Goes to Beijing; Newspaper Heiress Robs Bank; Mao Tse-Tung Dies.*

In some of my quiet moments—at night, mostly—when the playlot was dark, and the boys were all in their own homes, I wondered at the silence of our parents over the closing of the Wallace Playlot. I wondered where they were when the first blue machine clawed its fist into the outfield. For what did they stand if not this? Was it the price we paid for the gift of being left alone on all those summer afternoons? For the Wallace Playlot was a parentless place. From the first hint of afternoon to the pearly light of dinnertime, we learned to play there. Away from the custody of mothers and fathers, we learned to spit for distance and accuracy, how to scrape our knees and not cry, to take a punch and stay standing, how to let blood dry in the sun, and to swear like Gus Valenti and his punk friends who pitched nickels in front of the bakery. And under the suns of hundreds of afternoons we learned how to play softball. We learned how to throw the ball to the cut-off guy, how to hit to the opposite field, how to stretch a single into a double, how to keep the force-out alive.

But for some of us, the toughest lesson to learn was how to catch a softball.

Our instruction began in the outfield, where we were protected by space and time from the thud of the ball off the bat. We learned to catch it in our bellies first. When the ball came to us–if we were lucky–it slammed against our bellies, and we closed our hands around it. Everyone began that way, but the good players teased us, called us "belly catchers," and *bellycatchers* we remained until that unforgettable day when we learned to catch the ball in our hands alone. Nothing but hands. And if we learned the lesson, we learned it on our own, not from fathers who came home after work and explained the notions of eye-hand coordination, but from self-imposed determination, the unspoken discipline of wrapping our fingers around a softball countless times each day, and the endless negotiation of mistake and correction.

And when that momentous summer afternoon finally arrived, when the sun and wind were just right, when the ball hung just right, when all this just rightness converged with courage, and we finally decided *not* to anticipate the speed and direction of the ball in order to catch it in the glove of our bellies, but decided to reach within for the pluck necessary to run to the place where the ball might hit you in the nose if you failed, and we stretched our arms toward the sky, and at the last second opened our fingers, and finally felt the spiny seam of the ball slap against our hands, and we fastened our ten fingers around it and the negotiation ended unmistakably with correction, only then did we shed the name "belly catcher."

The softballs were sixteen inches around, with smooth, leathery shells, and we called them by the name stamped on every one: Clinchers. They cost three bucks, and out of the box they were as hard as plywood. They softened after a few innings, and by the end of summer, we had a canvas sack of two dozen balls, the newer ones hard enough to break a finger, and the older ones soft enough to sleep on.

And of all the boys in Bridgeport, of all the boys in Chicago, and maybe the world—I, Petey Bellapani, was the last one who learned to catch a softball at the Wallace Playlot. And this is how I learned.

We had just finished a pick-up game, and a dozen of us sat around drinking sodas from Bernie's Corner Store. Timmy Halloran held a bat in each hand, tapping a softball from one barrel to the other. Matty Vaccarello tried it, too, but it was harder than it looked, and he gave up and watched Timmy instead. Kenny Metke was wiping the playlot dirt from a softball in his hands, and Wundy Arrigo sat, elbows on his knees, and added spit to a puddle he was working on. Ronny Frugoli scraped the cork from inside the cap of his bottle of RC Cola and uncovered a ten-cent winner. He smiled, and Charlie Puffer said, "You got a winner?" And Ronny said, "Fuckin' ay, I got a winner," and Charlie said, "You ain't got a winner," and Ronny said, "Fuck you, Charlie. I got a winner," and Charlie shut up. We called Ronny "The Goat," which stood for The Greatest of All Time, because that's what he told us to call him.

Charlie curled his lips, blowing air into his Pepsi bottle. He made a musical tone after every drink he took, and when the note reminded him of a song he knew, he'd sing it out loud. After one note he broke into "The Hymn of the St. David's Marines," a song he had written the lyrics for.

> *From the halls of Saint David's*
> *To the fields of Bosley,*
> *We will fight our school's battles*
> *In softball and hockey.*
> *First to fight for the All-Saints trophy,*
> *Then to keep our white shirts clean.*

*We are proud to bear the title*
*Of The Saint David's Marines.*

Matty Vacc joined in with a forced bass, too deep for a boy, and Wundy Arrigo tried to sing along, too, but he couldn't do anything with a straight face except play sports, so he just tilted his head back and laughed. He laughed in church like that, too. Couldn't stop.

All around, Wundy was the best softball player at the lot. His real name was Denny, but during the Fourth of July all-star game that year, he hit three triples and a grand slam for a total of ten runs batted in. He threw three players out at the plate, too, and made a diving stab of a line-shot that might have turned the game around. Elmer Vulich was there. He was our age and he never played sports—something was wrong with him—but he announced all of our games from the stands like he was Howard Cosell—and as Denny rounded third base for his grand slam, Elmer called him *Mister Wonderful*. And that's what we called him for a while before we shortened it to *Wundy*.

Charlie and Matty followed their performance of the hymn of the St. David's Marines with a whistled verse of the fight song, and Wundy tried to whistle along, but he just laughed and blew out air and mists of spit.

That's when Kenny Metke spoke and started the whole thing. He looked straight at The Goat and said, "You throw any ball in that sack at me, and I'll catch it with one hand."

A riot of voices exploded, for though Kenny seemed to have directed his challenge to The Goat, he had not put anyone's name to it, and at the Wallace Playlot, a challenge like that belonged to everyone.

"I'm talking about you at shortstop, me at the plate," he said as he panned the lot of us. "You make a good throw. I catch it. One hand."

Kenny Metke was born a shortstop on the first day of summer in the year of our Lord, 1959. Even in pick-up games, only the best of us played shortstop—it was the front line of battle, where Clinchers shot at you like cannonballs. He played for Joe Harris Hardware—the perennial powerhouse of the Wallace Softball League. Kenny was the best ball handler in Bridgeport. He was three years older than me—thirteen that year—and he was like a man.

When the clamor following Kenny's challenge faded, it was agreed that there would be four throwers: Timmy Halloran, Charlie Puffer, The Goat, and Wundy. They were four of the biggest guns in the neighborhood, players just a summer or two away from breaking into the men's leagues at McGuane Park.

I dragged a bat handle in the dirt to make a circle for the throwers and then walked over to first base with Matty Vacc, where we could watch the thing unfold. We were giddy.

The Goat told Timmy Halloran to go first. Timmy matched Kenny pound for pound and could throw a Clincher a mile. He used a bigger baseball bat than anyone, and his back was like a capital *V.* From the circle, Timmy looked at Kenny and held the ball in the air out of respect.

"The game begins," he said, and Wundy laughed at the formality.

Timmy pumped his arm back and threw the ball with three-quarter speed, like a routine grounder to a first baseman you could count on. With a slap, Kenny's right hand covered the Clincher like a talon. He came out of his crouch, smiling, and returned the ball to Timmy.

"The game begins, indeed," Kenny repeated, and Wundy laughed again.

The Goat held a softball in each hand and looked from one to the next as he squeezed them for hardness. He kept the newer one and tossed the other to the ground. He glared at Kenny, who shut both hands sharply into fists and then splayed them open, hard and wide, preparing for The Goat's throw. The Goat toed the dirt at his feet, then slow-twisted his left foot into the ground as if he were crushing a bug. He pulled his right arm back like an archer drawing a bow and let his Clincher fly hard and fast. It shot toward Kenny's right shoulder, but Kenny crossed his body with his left hand, and shut it like teeth around the ball. The Goat growled and punched at the air.

"Fuckin' punk," he growled through his teeth. "Goddamn *lefty* he catches it."

Kenny couldn't hide a smile. He rolled the ball back as if The Goat didn't deserve a return throw, and Charlie lined up next. He still couldn't get "The Hymn of the St. David's Marines" out of his hum. Behind him, Wundy smiled and picked up another ball.

Kenny nailed Charlie's throw with his right hand and made a face like he was impressed with Charlie's effort. He raised his left arm at an angle toward the sun to hold off the throwers for a moment and pulled out of his crouch. He stood full, keeping his eyes on Timmy, and called my name.

"Petey!"

Still holding Charlie's first throw, Kenny flicked his right hand at me and nodded at the boys in the circle. Without a word, I understood that I was to receive the balls from Kenny and return them to the throwers so Kenny could concentrate on catching. He flipped Charlie's ball toward me, and it rolled to my feet. I picked it up and threw it to Charlie, and Kenny winked at me. I was in the game.

Kenny prepared himself, then, for Wundy's throw. It whisked in, swift and sharp, harder than any Clincher yet. Kenny clenched his teeth and grunted as he slapped his hand around the ball, and Wundy laughed.

Kenny rolled the ball to me, and by the time it reached my feet, another had been thrown and become trapped in his hand. As soon as that one rolled from his fingertips, another was rifled at him, and then they came like bullets strafed from the arms of four big boys. Left and right Kenny caught them. Matty Vacc started counting out loud after each slap of a ball in one of Kenny's hands.

*Slap.* "Thirteen."

*Slap.* "Fourteen."

I joined Matty as he counted.

*Slap.* "Fifteen."

A young mother, pushing her newborn in a stroller, stopped at the sidewalk along the left field foul line.

*Slap.* "Sixteen."

At "Eighteen" I stared at Kenny. Down the backs of his long hands, veins jiggled like night crawlers, and his skin stretched white over the bones. It was a marvel to me how his fingers clamped around each ball so definitely, and I could believe, then, that his hands were made for this, and this alone—that God had seen this very moment thirteen years before—had maybe even held a Clincher in His own holy fingers in the heaven of 1959, and considered the excellent idea of Kenny's hands.

At "Twenty-one" I followed his fingers down to his hands and to the thick lines of his forearms and up the pumping curves of his biceps, past his shoulders to his face, and was struck by the look in his eyes. They seemed strange and wild. If you didn't know him, you might have thought he was crazy. From the time the boy-men chose their softballs, Kenny's eyes locked on each one. It seemed he saw these Clinchers as none of us had ever seen them, as though each of them floated at him in slow motion. His eyes could even tell, I thought, from the particular gray of each softball, and from the way it turned and shifted in the air, how soft or hard each one would be. Perhaps his eyes could even see how the Clinchers altered the rills of aroma wafting from Dressel's Bakery across the street.

Staring at him then, as he fastened his glare to the path of each Clincher, I knew that catching softballs had something to do with this—with never looking away. I thought that if you took your eyes off the ball for the tiniest piece of an instant, you might no longer understand where it was and what changing space and time it occupied. If you did not always have your eye locked on it, you might lose it to the world. It made such sense: keep your eye on the ball. How many times had I heard that? But maybe it was an unteachable thing, and until you saw it work, until you really saw it as a thing of truth, it couldn't be known. But I knew it then.

As I stared at Kenny's eyes, and felt myself tightening my lips and making his same bug-eyed faces, as I squeezed my hands with the slapping sound of every catch, I knew that I would never take my eyes from another ball. That I would live a hundred summers or more and would never be called a bellycatcher again.

At "Twenty-three," the pace of the game picked up, and I nodded to Matty Vacc to give me a hand. He substituted for me while I took stock of the crowd that had begun to form on the edges of the playlot. Mr. Augle, the baker at Dressel's, leaned against the garbage can off third base, standing next to Mr. Barone, who cooked the annual spaghetti dinner for the Men's Club at St. David's. Mr. Augle's arms flinched, and his fingers tightened around an imaginary softball with every catch Kenny made.

Mrs. Pell, the crossing guard, stood on the other side of the backstop with her fingers knotted through the chain-link fence. At the end post of the backstop, on the third-base side, Elmer Vulich rocked anxiously, and his lips moved in the play-by-play going on inside his head.

By "Twenty-eight," I smiled with every slap of Kenny's hands around another Clincher. By "Thirty" I was laughing. Between throws, Timmy and the guys were laughing, too. Even The Goat. Did they still each hope, I wondered, to throw the ball that Kenny would drop?

The Clinchers kept coming.

When we closed in on the fiftieth throw, I wondered if they would stop there, and Kenny must have considered it, too, because at "Forty-seven" he screamed above the collective counting of the crowd, "Keep 'em coming!"

It left no room for doubt among anyone gathered there, but he screamed it again after "Forty-eight."

"I want a hundred! Keep 'em coming!"

It was as if he thought no one else was aware that a thing of some magnitude was happening, and he shouted it again after "Forty-nine."

"I want a hundred! Keep 'em coming!"

I laughed. I couldn't believe I was there.

*Slap.* "Fifty!"

This was like the big hit in the bottom of the seventh to save the game.

*Slap.* "Fifty-two!"

Like reuniting a lost child with its panic-stricken mother.

*Slap.* "Fifty-three!"

Like a fireman walking out of the black smoke of a burning building in slow motion with a crying baby in each arm.

*Slap.* "Fifty-four!"

This was the dive off the pier at Olive Park into Lake Michigan to save a drowning child.

*Slap.* "Fifty-five!"

Somewhere between "Fifty-six!" and "Sixty!" I looked toward Thirty-third Street, where Mr. Frugoli and Sergeant Halloran leaned against a squad car and spoke to each other between the screaming of numbers, their eyes fixed on their sons.

At "Sixty-five!" I noticed that traffic had completely stopped on Thirty-third Street. Cars were double-parked from Wallace to Parnell, and the streets were thick with the people of Bridgeport. They began to stream onto the outfield at "Sixty-eight!" Mr. Russo leaned on his cane holding a package from the bakery in his other hand.

*Slap.* "Seventy-two!"

It was like the crowd at the Fourth of July all-star game, and it seemed that everyone wanted Kenny to keep catching softballs, as if they wanted him not to fail, to never drop a ball, not on that day, or the next, or any day in his life from that day forward. It occurred to me that all of us–gunners, ball boys, passersby, double-parkers, store owners, nickel-pitching punks, city workers, purse snatchers, the punched and the punchers, too, that every man and woman in the neighborhood, from Bernie at the corner store, to Mickie "Bighead" Silvestri, to Mr. Augle, to Mayor Richard J. Daley himself, were tied to this game, and that its outcome would have something to say about all of us. It was as if the hope of the entire neighborhood— with its dozens of churches and hundreds of porches, with its Hamburg Club and Redwood Lounge, its Ramova Grill, and penny candy store, with its piles of unread newspapers filled with the world's undiscussed problems—the hope and promise of all of us, converged in and depended upon the huge, capable hands, and the unimpeachable eyes of a boy-man named Kenny Metke.

Where were the reporters and photographers now? I wondered. *This* was the headline I wanted to see: *KENNY METKE, SOME BOY!* And a color photograph of him crouched, huge hands in front of him, eyes burning holes in the camera. *This* was the front page I wanted to see when I delivered newspapers in the dark of the next morning.

Maybe it was the spirit of competition, or being on the verge of manhood, or maybe it was all they could do to throw with accuracy, but something kept The Goat, Charlie, Timmy, and Wundy throwing Clinchers with everything they had, as if anything less would be wrong.

Kenny was red faced and drenched with sweat by the time "Eighty-seven!" whipped through the air. He stared at it with bug-eyed verve and focus until it ended its journey in the claw of his hand.

The still growing assembly screamed the count that Matty Vacc had begun.

*Slap.* "Eighty-eight!"

*Slap.* "Eighty-nine!"

The Goat took a slow wind-up and rifled "Ninety!"

Charlie pumped "Ninety-one!" like a torpedo and Kenny's face twisted into something like fear when the Clincher nearly slipped from his sweat-covered hands.

Wundy picked up a ball for the next throw, but The Goat grabbed his arm on the wind-up so that Kenny could rest and dry his hands. Kenny stood and removed his soaking T-shirt. He screwed it into a tight knot, and sweat poured from it. The young mother strolled her newborn close to Kenny. She took a clean cloth diaper from her shoulder bag and handed it to him. He tossed his T-shirt in the dirt and took the cloth diaper, returning a "Thank you, ma'am," and after wiping his face, neck, and hands with the diaper, he turned toward the young mother, but she had retreated into the crowd. He set the diaper on home plate and returned to his crouch.

Wundy threw "Ninety-two!"

And that's when I felt, more than heard, from across the street and up three floors, the faint scream of my mother's call to dinner. It was translated by time and a half-block's distance into a whisper-scream, but still I knew, from the song of it, that it was the third time she had called. She wouldn't be pleased, but this was not just any day at the playlot, and anyone could see that some exception was necessary here.

And we of the playlot screamed, "Ninety-three!"

As Kenny snagged "Ninety-four!" I wanted the moment to never end. I wanted to take in the light and the dust and the spit and the zigzag seams of the balls and the cracks of the sidewalks, and the smells of the bakery, and the faces of the crowd, so that I would not forget this day.

By now, the cars had backed up along Wallace from Harris Hardware to the middle of the block. Along Thirty-third Street, men, women, and children were perched on every rooftop, attempting to make sense of why everyone in our world, from Chinatown to the Union Stockyards, was scream-counting in perfect unison. A fire truck was parked on the sidewalk along the third base foul line and a dozen kids had climbed on top to get a better look at the field. A fireman stood on the bumper of Engine #2 with a boy on his shoulders. Two squad cars flashed their lights to keep traffic from flowing down Thirty-third Street. In front of the hardware store, Eddie Bedore, our precinct captain, stood shoulder-to-shoulder with Joe Harris, both of them sucking on green cigars. Behind them, my father stood on the iron step of the store with his right hand against the bricks of the building, wearing his work blues and holding a thermos. Father Maloney had pulled his Volkswagen van onto the grass and three kids from St. David's camped on its roof.

Across the street, the sun set like a pearl over Dressel's Bakery; its lowest ripples danced on the short wall of the roof, and I knew the bakery loved this time of day.

I looked at the black fire escape, and followed it past the windows of our third floor apartment where dinner was soon to be served, past the swinging sign of the bakery to the entrance of the hallway, and there, framed in the doorway below her window, emerging from the black shadow of the stairwell, stood my mother.

The worry and anger I'd expected to accompany this rare fourth and final call vanished as she found Matty Vacc's mother at the bottom stair, and, having spotted their sons in the nave of the crowd–bloodless, safe, chaperoned by priests and policemen—they locked arms and walked across the street toward center field and joined what had become a group of mothers. *Our* mothers.

It was nearly dinnertime, and yet, undeniably, in this boys' arena made of dirt, spit, blood, and fence, our mothers kicked up low clouds of dust as they entered the sacred theater of us. Wiping their hands on aprons, slinging dishtowels over their shoulders, they joined us without hesitation or apology. They did not look angry. They did not scream our names to call us away. It was as if they, who had so often misunderstood the mysteries of boyhood, knew then that something was happening and that it wanted witness.

Their heads followed the slow-motion paths of the final Clinchers and their lips moved in slow-scream synchronization with the rest of the assembled crowd to form the words "Ninety-five!"

*Slap.* "Ninety-six!"

I laughed out loud to be a part of it all. In *our* playlot, there were mothers and fathers enough to field a league of their own. Some of them laughed, all of them smiled, and Mr. and Mrs. Metke seemed on the verge of something better still. And to all of them the setting sun gave glow.

I will tell you something about our mothers and fathers. They were not lawyers or consultants. They were not schoolteachers. They did not broker stocks or trade options. They were not college graduates. They did not send us away to summer camps or take us on high school visits. They did not protect us from the belly punches that punks threw at us from time to time. They did not buy us gifts on impulse while shopping. They did not talk to us about President Kennedy or Vietnam or the Symbionese Liberation Army. And until that August day in the summer of 1972, I am not sure they had ever set foot on the dirt of the Wallace Playlot.

Yet here they were: mothers who baked bread and sewed curtains, fathers to whom I delivered newspapers, men and women who worked with their hands and watched us through windows, who took us to church, and made us dress up on Sundays, mothers and fathers who dreamed and prayed, who cried sometimes, and made love in the dark. And in 1972, in a place called Bridgeport, in a city called Chicago, this is how they loved us.

On one of the final days of the final summer of the Wallace Playlot, in a yellow dirt garden where boys grew, I learned to catch a softball while watching Kenny Metke. And when Wundy Arrigo, laughing, threw the one hundredth ball high into the azure sky, a thousand eyes followed it from the setting sun into the palm of Kenny Metke's right hand, and every mother and father we ever knew laugh-screamed "One Hundred!" and in a secret part of their hearts, they knew how it felt to be a boy.

# The Hills of Laura

It is true that I hated Hucker Norton. But I didn't mean to crush his thumb.

He wasn't one of us. Even his name told you he was from some other place. We were Petey and Ronny and Davy and Matty, and he was Hucker. And it wasn't lost on us that he rhymed with *fucker*.

His answer to every question was, "Your mother." When a passing car beeped its horn and I asked, "Who was that?" Hucker told me it was my mother, and she was beeping at *him*. When we played cards and I asked the dealer what was wild, Hucker told me that it was my mother who was wild. By the time he'd been around for a month he'd learned all our mothers' names, and he called us by them. He called me *Mary*.

I used to wonder would girls treat each other like that, would they say to each other, "Your daddy," or "Your daddy's wild." I wondered if they called each other by their fathers' names, if they called each other Eddie, and Vince, and Anthony. But we were boys, and that was the thing about us, we allowed for such sins. We didn't hang around with Hucker Norton because he was friendly or because he'd always been there. We hung around with him because he was a boy.

It is also true that my tenth summer, the summer of 1972, began with a punch in the belly from Hucker Norton; my hands still clutch at my stomach when I think of it. Still, I could not have crushed his thumb for hate.

It was September and we were at the old Wallace Playlot, where holes had been clawed like scars in the yellow dirt garden that had grown boys into men for a hundred years until that summer. I stood on the foundation wall of the first home under construction, and held a cinder block in my trembling fingers. Below me, where the basement floor would be, was Hucker. He was crouched over, examining something in the dirt. I remember looking at my hands. I could see the white of every bone of them, and I was thinking how I'd never held a heavier thing, and then I felt the grit of the gray brick slip away from me, felt it scrape away from my skin like a thirty-pound block of sandpaper. I had no time to warn him.

My best friend, Matty Vaccarello, called it, "A spectacular act of negligence." He was eleven years old, nearly twelve, and he was there when it happened, and I swear to God that's how he talked. If you told him about something that happened, he would listen closely, and ask questions about what you'd seen, who was there, and what they did, and all of a sudden you'd be telling him how you *felt* about what happened. And when you were done telling him, he would put his own words to the thing that happened, he would retell the story better than you, and then he would look you in the eye, and he'd wait for you to say something like, "Yes! That's it! That's exactly what I felt!" That's what Matty did, he took the slop and mess of our words and made them into truths that couldn't be denied.

Matty Vacc saw it all: how the cinder block plummeted from my hands and smashed onto Hucker's, and how Hucker screamed, and then how he climbed up the stairs we'd constructed of wood scraps and brick—still screaming—and how he ran home without looking back at us. And all I could do was stare at Matty after Hucker left.

"It was an accident, Matty," I finally said. "I didn't mean it."

And Matty looked me in the eye and he didn't say anything, he just looked at me, and then he looked at the blood on the ground below us. He kept shaking his head on our way back to his house, and when we finally got there, he asked me a hundred questions; and after I told him everything, he looked at me and didn't say anything for a while. He just nodded his head and chewed on the inside of his cheek, and when he finally spoke, what he called it was, "A spectacular act of negligence."

But that night, lying awake in bed, when the shock of Hucker's scream finally wore off, and when I could close my eyes and not see the blood and the look on Hucker's face, what I was thinking was something I hadn't told Matty. What I was thinking was that we were *even*, Hucker and me. He'd punched me in the stomach to start the summer, and I'd crushed his thumb to end it.

On the day of the punch, three months earlier, it was the same three of us, it was me and Hucker and Matty again. We were in front of Dressel's Bakery, where I lived on the third floor, and Hucker was standing where a punk named Gus Valenti had etched the words, *Fuck you Mary Nelson 1970,* into the once-wet cement.

I'm not certain why Hucker punched me; it might have been something like a dare, because Matty said something to me later, about how I must have tapped into the violent psyche of Hucker Norton. Hucker might have been telling a story about how he punched some kid by his cousin's house, he was always talking about how he punched somebody, or how he stole something from the store, or hit a home run, or found twenty bucks, or kissed a girl; and maybe I was just tired of the stories, and I rolled my eyes and said, "Yeah, right, Hucker." And then maybe he said, "You wanna make a bet I did, Mary? You want me to prove it?"

And that *is* what I wanted. Proof. I wanted a photograph of the punch, or I wanted someone like Matty to tell me he was there and it was true because he saw it happen. Proof was what

I wanted. It was the only thing to keep me from falling for a lie, which was the worst kind of falling. I didn't want to be laughed at for believing a thing that wasn't true: I wanted to be savvy and smart, I wanted to smell a lie from a mile away, to be able to look a kid in the eye and know for certain that what he said was true. But I couldn't do that. I couldn't smell the difference between lies and the truth. So, without thinking, maybe I said something like, "Yeah, Hucker, why don't you prove it."

And before I had a chance to think about what I said— before I had a chance to drag back my stupid dare, or whatever it was, Hucker moved into his wind-up, reached all the way back. I still thought he was bluffing, that he was going to fake like he was going to punch me, just to make me flinch—he was always trying to make somebody flinch—but when he turned toward me again, he had a look on his face I'd never seen, his teeth were shut hard against each other and his lips were pulled tight across his teeth, and it looked like he had muscles everywhere, even in his forehead and cheeks; and all of a sudden it didn't seem like he was lying anymore about punching this kid, he had a stance and a wind-up and a swing path, and it seemed as though they'd all been used before. And in one explosive second, his swing ended with a hard-fisted shock to my belly, and it seemed as though the world had flipped over on me. In the instant of the punch, it seemed the world had become a different place. I was a punched boy. I wasn't even sure I was a boy anymore.

I did not fall. Nor did I stumble. Hucker would have seen this if he had stayed. He would have seen me clutch at my stomach, would have seen my body fold forward and my mouth open wide to let in air. He would have heard me gasp–struggling to breathe, wanting and wanting not to cry, and he would have known, then, that these were not only the sounds of a boy who'd just been punched, but they were the sounds of a boy who was beginning to believe. But before I could breathe or cry or lift my head to see anything more than the message Gus Valenti had left for Mary Nelson, Hucker had turned away from Matty and me, had jaywalked across the street and past the old Wallace

Playlot, thinking, perhaps, that he'd taught me a lesson. I'd wanted proof, and he'd given me what I'd asked for.

But I wonder now if it might have been something else that I wanted. Maybe I didn't want proof that it was true at all. Maybe what I wanted was proof that it *wasn't* true. Maybe I didn't want to believe the world was a place where a ten-year-old boy could find a reason to punch. And maybe I didn't want to believe that boys hit home runs or found money or kissed girls, because if I believed they did those things, then maybe it was proof that nothing ever happened to me, that all around me boys were being heroes, they were being cheered and honored and kissed, that I was standing still while an unbelievable world was going on without me. And so I played it safe. I didn't believe any of it. I refused to believe anything, unless I saw it happen, unless I did the thing myself.

With Matty Vacc, though, there wasn't the wondering, because he wasn't a puncher and he wasn't a cheater, and he insisted on the truth of things. But three years after the summer of the punch and the cinder block, when he told me what happened while he was with Laura Fantano in his basement, he gave me something to think about. We'd all been kissed by then—even me. But this time—if I was to believe Matty—was different.

"So I'm sitting in my dad's office in his swivel chair," Matty said. "And Laura's on my lap, and we're kissing. And after a while she stops kissing me and looks me right in my eyes," he said. "She reached behind her back and slipped her hands under her T-shirt to unhook the clasp of her bra."

Matty went back and forth from the present to the past, as if he wasn't happy with the question of tense.

"Her shoulder pointed toward me like this," and Matty reached back like he was unclasping his own bra. "And she was still looking right at me, Petey. Then she slips her right arm back through her T-shirt sleeve, and then she slips it through again, and then she tucks her right hand under her shirt and then I think she did something with her left arm, she tucked it back through her sleeve or something—I don't know what the hell she did—and anyway, out comes her bra through her sleeve like magic. And when she did that, her 'breasts,' that's what he called them, he called them *breasts*, "I felt like I knew what they were going to look like, and how they would *feel*...It was like I had a *sense* of them."

Matty made all these dreamy and sexy faces while he was telling me the story, like he was Laura Fantano herself, and I just listened to him. I was thinking about Laura, who lived right across the street from me, next to Morrissey's Roofing Company, and I couldn't believe she'd let a boy see her breasts. It made me wonder about all the girls I knew, but I didn't say, "Yeah, right, Matty." I didn't say he was full of shit, and there was no eye-rolling, or anything, because he'd never told me anything like this before, and on the chance that it was true I let him finish.

"Then she lifts her T-shirt above her breasts...And Petey," he said, "It *stayed* there. Just like it was sitting on a little shelf, and she closed her eyes and brought her hands to mine. She traced her fingers over mine and lifted my hands, and then she brought them to her breasts, and it was like a dream. It was like we were all grown up, the way she took my hands in hers and whispered them across her skin." That's what he said, that "she *whispered* his hands across her skin."

"And there they were, Petey, Laura's breasts. In these very hands. They were perfect," he said. "They were..." And Matty closed his eyes. He needed to put Laura's breasts into words that I would believe. He closed his eyes, and he held out his hands, palms facing me, as if he couldn't find the words in his head to compare to breasts, but maybe he could find them with his hands.

"Little hills, they were, Petey. The hills of Laura," he said, and he opened his eyes, and he looked at me to see if I understood, but I guess he could tell that I didn't. He could see that he hadn't gotten at the truth of Laura's breasts.

Then his face lit up and he smiled, and he looked at the shape of his hands as they held the memory of Laura.

"You know what it felt like, Petey? It felt like holding my hand out the car window to feel the wind on the highway."

And then Matty laughed, and he put his right hand out as if he were in the passenger side of his father's car. He laughed as though he'd found the exact truth of Laura's breasts. He laughed as if he was certain that this was the thing I most needed to know in order to understand. Then Matty opened his eyes and looked at me again.

"Know what I'm talking about, Petey?" he said. "On the highway? When the air shapes your hands like this? Well if you close your eyes and think of a girl, it's like she's right there. You oughta try it, Petey," he said. "When you're in the car with your dad you oughta give it a shot."

I felt my fingers twitch.

"I'll never forget it," he said. "It was like holding the wind in my hands."

I wanted to believe Matty. *This* was the world I wanted to live in—one in which a girl's T-shirt rested on the shelf of her breasts for a boy to see, a world in which a girl sat on a boy's lap and whispered his fingers across her skin. I hadn't actually seen him touch Laura's breasts, though, and who knew how long it would be before I had a girl with breasts of her own. But my father had a car. And there was always the wind.

My father made deliveries for Dressel's Bakery, and that Saturday morning we filled the back seat of our sky-blue Pontiac Catalina with a small wedding cake and bags of bread fresh from the oven, and pulled out of the parking lot behind the bakery. We made two stops on Taylor Street and headed toward Harrison, where we swung onto the Eisenhower Expressway for the next delivery. I'd been thinking about Laura's breasts since the minute I woke up, but we'd covered almost a mile of highway before I got up the nerve to take hold of them. I kept looking at my dad.

At Western Avenue I put my hand on the armrest of the door, and inched my fingers toward the window. I set my wrist on the window slot and let my fingers play with the wind, let the wind run across the tips of my fingers. I reached out a couple of inches more and the wind breathed on my wrist, and then I stretched my hand out further, but the second it cupped the full wind of the highway, I got scared and I whipped my hand back into the car, and looked at my father, but he hadn't noticed a thing. He'd turned the radio on and was fiddling with the tuner at the staticky end of the dial. He must have felt me looking at him, though, because he turned to me and winked. I smiled and looked straight ahead. I wasn't sure how long we were going to be on the Eisenhower, so when he turned back to look at the road I just slipped my hand out the window again, like it wasn't a big deal or anything, like I was just putting my hand out the window, and then my hand held the wind, or the wind held my hand, and I think it was September, because there was nothing like September in Chicago, and the wind was cool in my hand, but I felt the heat of the sun, too. I closed my eyes. I let the wind be the wind, let it work against my fingers; I gave my fingers to it.

I wanted to look at my hand, to see the shape of it, but I was afraid if I looked, it would be like waking up from a dream of a bag of money to find that it's gone, so I didn't look. But it felt like the wind was shaping it into something that really was like breasts. And as my hand danced with the wind, I imagined Laura's face, her brown eyes and the way her hair fell into her eyes, and the way her cheeks dimpled when she smiled. I couldn't help it. I tried to think of another girl, because Laura was Matty's girl, and so I thought of Bridget Pentecoff, who'd just moved in down the street. She was beautiful and her hair was like six white crayons and one yellow one, melted together. I pressed my eyelids together and tried to think of Bridget, which, any other time would have worked, but Laura's T-shirt and the shelf of her breasts kept coming back, so I stopped trying to think about Bridget, and when I heard my father start to sing I turned my head toward him and opened my eyes, still careful not to look at my hand.

He'd just tuned into a radio station at the start of a Tony Bennett song, and he smiled, as if the day couldn't get any better. He was singing along with Tony Bennett and I looked ahead at the highway and smiled, because Tony Bennett was the perfect thing to be on the radio just then; because I only saw my father cry twice in my life, and I don't know why he was crying one of those times, but the other time was when Tony Bennett was on television singing a song. I don't remember what song it was, but my father started singing along with Tony, and all of a sudden he had to stop because he was crying, but he was kind of laughing, too. But on the radio in the car that Saturday, it was "Fly Me to the Moon" that Tony Bennett was singing, and my father was singing along with him and he wasn't crying. He was smiling and holding his pocket comb like it was a microphone and he was singing,

> *Fly Me to the Moon,*
> *Let me play among the stars,*
> *Let me see what spring is like*
> *On Jupiter and Mars...*

And he didn't sound bad, my father, and I smiled because I think I could've done anything in the car and it would've been all right, I could've lit a cigarette in the car and he probably would've let me sit there and smoke. I could've blown smoke rings in his face, and he probably would have laughed and poked his fingers through the smoke rings, and kept right on singing, so I just closed my eyes and shoved my other hand out the window, too. I put it out there like it was nothing, and the wind from the highway swirled the smell of warm bakery bread around the car, and I think I could even see the smells swirling, and the heat of the sun felt like warm hands on my face and my neck, and I knew for a fact that what Matty told me was true.

And maybe everything else was true, too. Maybe there

were boys who punched, and hit homeruns to win the game, and maybe there were girls who kissed and lifted their shirts, and whispered the fingers of boys over their breasts, and maybe I should never have lifted a cinder block in my hands with Hucker so close. Maybe I should have been more careful.

But that Saturday I was thirteen years old, and my dad was singing "Fly Me to the Moon," and my hands cupped the September wind and everything felt so good I almost laughed out loud. And then I opened my eyes. I opened my eyes because it felt so real I was sure that nothing would disappear, nothing would go away just for the opening of my eyes. And I looked at my hands in the shape of Laura Fantano's breasts, and behind them the trees on the side of the highway they were a blur. We were going so fast.

# The Pilgrim Virgin

All of these things about Gus Valenti were true. He pitched nickels in front of our apartment above Dressel's Bakery, and didn't budge an inch when people passed. He sat on the hoods of other people's cars smoking cigarettes, and flicking his butts into the street. He spit through his teeth and swore like a Teamster. He didn't work. There may have been other reasons why my father hated Gus, but it seemed as though these were enough. What my father did not know is that it was Gus—three years before—who had etched *fuck you Mary Nelson, 1970* in the wet cement at the entrance to our stairwell.

I had stood guard over the newly poured cement that day, an eight-year-old sentinel, had watched as Gus authored the words that would greet me every day as I walked from the darkness of the stairwell into the days of my boyhood. I sometimes chanted the words under my breath like a litany. The short song of the curse would disappear for a while, and return without warning as I delivered newspapers, or sat in church; or it would come to me at school while I stared emptily at the chalkboard.

I never told my father it was Gus who vandalized the cement, even though he asked me several times, "Are you sure, Petey?" I was positive. I told him it was some other guy, bigger than Gus.

My father didn't need another reason to hate the punk; by the time 1973 rolled around, the list was three years long.

When he saw me alone, though, Gus called me *Petey Bee*, and winked at me. He'd say, "Gimme skin, Petey Bee," and I'd slap my hand onto his palm and slide it across. Or he'd muss my hair on the way up to his apartment on the floor below ours. I was eleven then and these things meant something.

In my father's eyes, the leaning and smoking and cursing added up to something like sin, and tumbled together with the unforgivable fact that Gus was a teenager. It might have been forgivable if my father had ever been a teenager himself, but I think he skipped from twelve to twenty without going through his teens.

There is one picture of my father from his youth. It's a black and white photograph and he's sitting at a piano, looking over his shoulder at the camera as if he'd been caught off guard. His face is smooth and his hair is black and rich, but something in his face—his unsmiling eyes, maybe, or the tightness in his lips—belies his youth. Even at fifteen he looked like a man.

What made it worse, was that it seemed Gus had no idea my father didn't like him. He called my father "Joe" when he saw him. "Hey, what's up, Joe," he'd say, and I would cringe. In my father's clenched face I could see that he wanted to grab a handful of Gus's dago-tee and rapid-pump his fist against Gus's chest, pushing him against somebody's car—perhaps even our own Catalina, until Gus folded over backwards on the hood and maybe even felt something crack in his lower back. My father would knock the Marlboro out of Gus's mouth with a slap that would brush against his lips, and say, *Listen punk! Who the fuck do you think you're calling 'Joe? I bust my ass working two jobs while you sit out here on the hard-earned property of good people and smoke your goddamn Marlboros and pitch your goddamn nickels! My name is Mister Bellapani, you fuckin punk! Mis-Ter-Bel-La-Pa-Ni!* A pump of his fist against Gus's chest with every syllable of the name that belonged to me as well.

But my father didn't swear, and even if he did, I was certain he'd never say *goddamn*. He clung, like an obedient child, to the misshapen golden rule that 'if you can't say something nice about somebody, keep your mouth shut.' So he kept his mouth shut, my father did, and he shut up his hatred, too, along with his lesser iniquities, clutched his sins like secrets to keep them venial. And he'd return Gus's "What's, up Joe?" with a nod, or a stern, mumbled response that was more sound than word, but if you listened carelessly, it might actually have sounded like "How you doing?" I knew what it was, though. It was a way for my father to hate Gus in secret.

I would turn around and look back at Gus, then, with a sort of shrug apology, and my father would put his arm on my shoulder and turn me from my backward glance, like he was moving a checker to a more protected square. Gus would nod his head in my direction and wink, as if we had a shared something.

November began that year, as it always did, with a week—long visit from the Virgin Mary—a shining white statue brought to us by the Guardians of the Pilgrim Virgin—three Sicilian men who carried her to fifty-two homes in the course of a year, where she'd stand solemnly on makeshift altars so that her adoring faithful could pray the rosary before her.

My mother laid a lacy runner, bleached white and ironed starchy smooth, across the buffet table, and the Guardians positioned the Virgin in its center. And there, Mother Mary, full of grace, hands folded in prayer, stood before us. A notice in the St. David's bulletin invited parishioners to our house at seven o'clock every night where they could kneel for hours to reflect on the Sorrowful, Joyful, and Glorious Mysteries of the lives of Mary and Jesus.

On the day the Guardians dropped off the Pilgrim Virgin, one of the men led the rosary, but on the other days my father would lead. He would begin each *Our Father and Hail Mary* solo and hold to his lines like a priest:

> *Our Father who art in Heaven*
> *Hallowed be thy name.*
> *Thy Kingdom come,*
> *Thy will be done,*
> *On earth as it is in Heaven...*

Halfway through, the assembled, kneeling in a half-circle, would chime like a choir:

> *Give us this day*
> *Our daily bread,*
> *And forgive us our trespasses,*
> *As we forgive those*
> *Who trespass against us.*
> *And lead us not into temptation*
> *But deliver us from evil, Amen.*

The blessed hum of the rosary in my living room was something to hear. You could sleep like a baby to its music if it weren't for the hell brought on by an hour's kneeling. By the second decade of the rosary, my knees would be red and sore, and I'd shift my weight from one to the other every few seconds without relief. In the front of the room, close enough to touch the Virgin, my father would kneel, straight as a crucifix, as if he'd stay in that position for days if he thought it might save some poor soul in purgatory.

Between each decade of the rosary, after the last *Hail Mary* and *Glory Be*, we would recite the *Oh My Jesus* as one voice:

> *Oh my Jesus, forgive us our sins.*
> *Save us from the fires of hell.*
> *Lead all souls into Heaven*
> *Especially those in most need of Thy mercy.*

Save us from the fires of hell. To say it was to have the thing done, it seemed. If there were such a thing as the fires of hell, I thought the Oh My Jesus might have been prayer enough to save us from them.

At the end of the week, when the Guardians returned to pick up the Pilgrim Virgin, they would give us a bag of scapulars blessed by the Pope. Sacred reminders of the eternal presence of Mary, they were thin necklaces made of white string, with squares of cloth that hung from the front and back. An image of Mother Mary graced the front cloth, and a brown-ink message on the back promised that *Whosoever dies wearing this scapular shall never suffer eternal fire.*

And so, on Sunday, November 4, 1973, in the second year of my second decade of life, the Guardians of the Pilgrim Virgin, with their flaming hearts and steel knees, delivered the statue of the holy mother of Christ to our apartment. And so we prayed the rosary, and perhaps shortened the sentences of innumerable souls in purgatory. So too, perhaps, we credited time against our own sentences.

As it happened, though, the blessed scapulars never arrived at the end of that week. When the Guardians returned to our apartment above Dressel's Bakery to pray the rosary and to continue the Virgin's pilgrimage, they discovered a bakery that had burned to the ground.

In the early dark of Sunday, November 11, an electrical fire had started in the bakery's dairy refrigerator, two floors below our living room. It soared straight up the old plaster and lath walls of the building, blowing fire through every room of the bakery apartments.

I woke to the sound of fist and wood—the frenzied, muscled sound of hands battering against our wooden door. I heard screaming. In the seconds it took me to adjust to the rules of waking life, the screams were wordless, they were throaty and visceral and belonged to a man.

I don't know which of the sounds, the screaming or the banging, awoke my father. Perhaps he was busy twisting and shifting in tormented sleep; perhaps all of the things he kept in a fettered and secret place during the day had been set wild and free in his dreams. Maybe his dreams were overworked and beaten things, so that in the banging and screaming of that dark morning, his dreams, looking for a moment's rest, locked him into a fisted and violent narrative, until the sound of splintering wood, and the urgent smell of fire joined the fear-filled screams of my mother; and finally, too great to be contained by one dream, they pulled him in unprotected panic from his sleep. I stood frozen in the doorway of my bedroom, staring hollow-eyed at the flames climbing the living room curtains. The lace of the Pilgrim Virgin's altar burned and curled toward her like fingers. I should have my shoes during a fire, I was thinking, but I wasn't looking for them.

And from the screams came words.

"Fire! Get up, Joe! Fire!"

A hand grabbed my elbow and yanked me toward the doorless entrance of our apartment. On the way into the hallway, my bare foot banged against the top edge of the fallen door, and I had time to see, against the flames of the living room, the shadowed and panicked figures of my mother and father running from their dreams.

The man who held me screamed, "I got Petey!" and wrenched me into the dark stairwell. In the hallway the smoke was thin, like fog; it smelled of burned bread and old wood. Through the mists of smoke, three firemen appeared along the length of a fire hose they were snaking up the stairs. The hand moved up my arm and I felt carried, like in a dream. This is how we run in dreams, I thought. As we passed the firemen, each one stopped what he was doing for a second to look into my eyes. One of them winked at me. They nodded over my shoulder at the man who was guiding me. My feet touched four of the thirty-three stairs as I was carried toward the November night.

Outside, the pavement was cold under my feet. I was led across the street to where a crowd had gathered in front of the new houses that had replaced the Wallace Playlot. They must have heard the fire engines, I thought. When they heard the fire engines, they must have awakened with the same panic of fire, and they are relieved now to find their own houses safe. The air breathed cool. I warmed one foot on top of the other, and shifted every few seconds to relieve the cold, pavemented foot. I felt an arm on my shoulder and looked behind me. It was Gus Valenti. It was Gus whose hands had hammered the door, whose voice had screamed my parents awake, and who had taken me safely from my burning home. He wore blue jeans and a jean jacket over his dago-tee. Noticing my shifting feet, he said, "Oh, shit," and he took off his jacket and put it on the ground in front of me.

"Step on that, Petey Bee," he said, and he stooped to wrap my feet with his jacket like the skirt of a Christmas tree.

Across the street, great pillows of black smoke poured from the windows of the building. Tongues of fire shot through the smoke.

The sound of coughing came from the stairwell, then, and in the doorway was my mother. She had her arms wrapped around something white. A box. Our hamper. A fireman walked toward her and held his arms out to take the hamper, but she wouldn't let it go. Behind the hamper she wore a thin nightgown. She was looking around in a panic, her face red and swollen. She burst into tears when she saw me, and began to cross the street.

Minutes later, my father followed her, coughing out smoke as well. He was completely dressed for work. He wore his work blues, black shoes, fall coat, and black knit hat, as if he had prepared for this fire. In his arms he carried what I knew, by its shape, was the Pilgrim Virgin. It was covered with a blanket. As he stepped off the last wooden stair, the blanket began to slip away to reveal the Virgin's hands still shaped in prayer, and I wondered if she was heavy. I was thinking, my father saved the Virgin Mary from a fire.

I thought of the faded and worn, brown-ink promise on the

back of the scapular I still wore from the November before. I thought how Mary may have had the power to protect us from the fires of hell, but she couldn't do shit for us in a bakery fire. She stood with her hands folded and did nothing in a bakery fire. She stood on the buffet table watching the runner burn at her feet. She needed my father to protect her.

As my mother walked across the street toward us, Gus stood behind me with his right hand on my shoulder, a Marlboro cigarette burning in his other hand, and I thought of how close I was to Gus as he smoked a cigarette, and how we both stood in the sight of my father, and how my father had nothing to protect me from. If he said anything to me about being so close to Gus, I was going to tell him this, I was going to tell him, "Gus saved us, Dad. Gus saved all of us, even the Virgin Mary if you think about it, Dad," and I wondered if my father knew this even without me saying so.

My mother wasn't crying. She was weeping, and looking at me and Gus as she walked toward us.

She could do this, I thought. She could walk right up to us, me and Gus, in the middle of a cold, Bridgeport night, wearing only her nightgown and holding a hamper against her chest, crying and knowing everything. Knowing that we were all alive and that Gus had saved us all, and she could put her arms around both of us. She could do that, my mother.

But what would my father do? He'd hold his head high, and maybe open the back door of the Catalina Pontiac, placing the Virgin Mary across the back seat. He might even buckle the seat belt around her. He might walk to us and remove his coat and hold it up to my mother's back so she could slip her arms through its sleeves. He might even wrap the Virgin's blanket over my shoulders and nod to Gus. As if a nod were enough.

But what he couldn't do was walk across the street to us, empty his arms of the Virgin Mary, and fill them with the truth, and then hold it up, hold up the truth to all of us, to all the somnambulists of Bridgeport, all the fire watchers, the mothers, the sons, the cops, the priests, and the punks, and then tell it to

us all. Tell us only what was true: that the place he had tried
to make into a home was burning to the ground. He had done
his best to provide and to protect but he was not omnipotent, he
wasn't God, and he wasn't an angel, and he wasn't a fireman.
He was just a man. And a punk had saved his family.

I wanted him to look at Gus and to hold out his hand for
Gus to shake and maybe to hold out his mistake about Gus, too,
for everyone to see. Or maybe just look the fucking punk in the
eye and say Thank you. Thank you, Gus. That's all. So there
would be no doubt that my father was saying Thank you.

I would smile if he said that. Yes. Because I was just a boy,
and still I had always known that there was something to Gus.

And maybe Gus would say, *No problem, Mister Bellapani.*

As it happened, my father did not walk to our car to place the
Virgin Mary safely across the back seat. He stepped carefully
over the fire hose, and without looking up, turned to his left and
set the statue on the ground. The blanket slipped and fell to the
Virgin's sandaled feet. Without looking back, my father walked
to the curb and stepped into the street between our sky-blue
Catalina and the fire truck, looking both ways before crossing,
as if over his right shoulder there were no building on fire.
Behind him, the Pilgrim Virgin stood sentry, while behind her,
flames darted from the windows, and smoke poured in long,
black pillows. Yet she stood there unchanged, hands folded in
prayer.

As my father came closer, his eyes were swollen and red
from the smoke. Or maybe from something else. Maybe he
felt all those things a man feels as he exits the burning place he
called home, a place he'd been trying to grow into something,
a place he'd tried to protect, but could not. And maybe his eyes
carried the weight of the burning of those things.

Across the street stood the Pilgrim Virgin. I wondered if
she could feel the heat of the fire behind her. I wondered if,
from the corner of her eye, she could see the message to Mary
Nelson that Gus had long ago etched in the once-wet cement.

Or if she could see my father as he stood still in the middle of
the northbound lane, trembling, as if he weren't certain of so
many things.

# Mrs. Higgins's Heart and The Smell of Fire

The second that Edward Higgins opened his eyes to the world he sprang from his bed and into the kitchen. He squinted at the clock on the wall.

"Yes." He whispered the word, and pumped his fist to it. It was 2:17.

Every morning for nearly a month—without explanation or exception—he'd been waking up at exactly 2:17. It had annoyed him at first, as it was difficult to return to sleep, but after a week of such wakings, the exactness had begun to fascinate him, so that his heart would race for a moment in fear that the clock might read 2:18 or 2:19, or a time even further from the mark.

So it was that on November 11, 1973, precisely because of this inexplicable drift in early-morning behavior, that Edward Higgins learned of the fire that would destroy the Bellapanis' apartment above Dressel's Bakery before the rise of the sun. On his way back to bed, Edward noticed the flashing lights of a fire engine spinning against the living-room curtains. Barefoot, he padded to the front of the house and opened the door, and saw, at the corner of Wallace and Thirty-third Streets, flames darting from the bakery windows.

"Holy Moses," he said. He counted the windows up from

the bakery to where the worst of the flames shot from the Bellapanis' third-floor apartment.

Edward had known Joe Bellapani since they were both in kindergarten at St. David's, and now, thirty years later, Ed's daughter, Sharon, was in the seventh grade with Bellapani's son, Petey.

He wondered if there was a way to keep his wife from knowing about the fire, but of course, it would have been impossible. He returned to his room and touched the back of his fingers to her cheek.

"Bertie, love," he whispered, and she woke with a start. "Don't be alarmed," he said. "There's a bit of a fire at the bakery. I'm going to check on the Bellapanis."

Mrs. Higgins sat up quickly and put her hand to her mouth.

"Bertie. I'm sure they're OK, sweetie. But I may return with them."

In one fluid motion, she whipped her blanket off and swung her legs over the edge of the bed. Edward put his hands to her shoulders.

"Honey, I'm sure they're fine. Maybe you should get the guest room ready. In case I come home with them."

Bertie Higgins had no doubt that her husband *would* return with the Bellapanis, for the moment he turned from her she had a vision of Mary Bellapani coming through her front door. She made the sign of the cross, and said "Let His love be on my mind, on my lips, and on my heart."

As the last word whispered from her lips, Bertie Higgins felt a sharp pain at her heart, for she had the quality of feeling, precisely, the pain of others. Her mother had called it a gift, but it had always been difficult for Bertie, even in prayer, to think in such terms. Gifts oughtn't hurt like this.

Though the pain worried Bertie greatly, she kept it secret for years. It was a school day, a Wednesday, when Bertie finally told her mother. She had taken the bus home from high school that day. For half of a block, she'd been watching a boy, a teenager, waiting at the corner for the streetlight to change. He was brown-haired and his face looked so soft and perfect, she thought she could almost feel the softness of his skin, and even as she watched him, she worried that something terrible might happen. It seemed to her that sound had stopped as she looked at the boy.

Bertie's bus pulled to the corner as the boy's light turned green, and sound returned. She turned her head quickly when she heard the racing engine of an automobile. Over her shoulder, a pea-green car sped toward the intersection from behind the bus as the boy stepped off the curb and into the street. Bertie closed her eyes, *knowing* the car would hit the boy, but she might as well have kept them open, so clearly did she see it. She shuddered with the boy's fear, she stiffened with the paralysis that froze him in the car's path. Bertie saw the car come at *her*, and screamed just before the sound, the terrible sound of bone and skin against metal. She felt a hammering at her femur. It seemed as though she were spinning in the air, and she was positive, even with her eyes closed, that the boy was spinning as well. She put her finger to her ear. She was certain it would be red with blood, as his would be. But it wasn't.

It was then she felt the pain at her breast. It was sharper than the other times. She shut her eyes against it, and twice her mouth opened at the shock of it. It felt as though she'd been shot in the heart—or stabbed—and under her blouse, she put her hand to her breast to keep her heart from breaking through. She checked her fingers for blood, but there was none. She had a headache, her pulse knocking against her temples from the inside, like knuckles, but it was nothing against the pain at her heart. She feared it would burst and although she'd promised herself to keep the pain a secret from everyone, it was so intense this time, she made a deal with God that if she made it home she'd tell her mother.

At home, Bertie greeted her mother with a hug and a flood of tears. It took a while to get to the point about the pain; every time Bertie began telling the story of the accident, she pictured

the boy—the way his hair flopped on his forehead—and began
again to cry. Her mother finally asked her to draw a diagram of
the accident, and the story finally came.

"I knew something bad was going to happen, Mom. If I
had been on the corner with the boy I would not have let him
cross the street."

When the crying ended this time, they held hands across
the dining room table, and prayed for the boy. And Bertie told
her mother about the stab at her heart.

"It happens all the time," she said. "On the bus I might
catch someone's eyes and I'll feel it. Or I'll be in line behind
someone at the store, an older man, buying a stack of TV
dinners, and it will happen again. Or I'll see an accident on
the highway."

Bertie paused and lifted her hand to her heart.

"Sometimes I look at Sister Marie during morning mass
and I'll feel it," she continued. "Today, with the boy, it was
worse, but usually it feels like..." Bertie cupped the palm of her
left hand and held it open. "...like someone has my heart in his
hand—my actual heart—and is flicking at it with his finger."

Having described it this way, it was difficult, whenever
the pain returned, for Bertie to forget the image of a fingernail
snapping at her heart.

Bertie did what she could to protect herself. She avoided
watching news on the television and listening to the radio. She
never read the papers. In the family car, she preferred the back
seat, where she was less likely to see accidents on the side of
the road. And when she married Edward, she began to keep
needlework projects in a box she kept in the car, and while they
traveled, she worked on them with great attention to detail.

Bertie wiped her eyes when the door closed behind Edward.
She took her robe from the bedpost and slipped it onto her arms.
Tying the sash around her waist, she knelt at the side of her bed.
She did not make the sign of the cross a second time, for once
she made it upon waking she felt she was within the parameters

of prayer, and here she lived each day.  Nor did Bertie close her eyes, for fear that fiery images would tumble through her prayer. She stared, instead, at the crucifix on the wall, focused on the mark where the ceramic arm of Jesus was glued to His shoulder. She kept her prayer brief, for there was water to be boiled for tea, there were rooms to be straightened.  And to concentrate on prayer with so much to do in so little time was to deny God the attention He deserved.  Soon, she lifted herself from her knees, and began to prepare for the Bellapanis.

She flitted from room to room in a kind of cleaning frenzy: fluffing pillows, wiping dust from the tops of dressers and the frames of wall hangings.  She vacuumed, swept, and polished– all to an untraceable logic. Bertie was a project skipper.  Though her home was unimpeachably clean, her housekeeping method was a stream of unpredictable steps, linked in a way  only she could explain.  Mr. Higgins found this behavior a source of infinite entertainment.  He'd sit on the couch with Sharon at his side, and while they pretended to watch television they'd quietly amuse themselves with a game they called The Bertie Higgins Play-by-Play.

"Aaaaaaaand there she goes," he'd whisper to Sharon. "She takes the vacuum cleaner to the living room carpet.  Edges it against the coffee table, where she looks at the framed family photos.  Oh, she sees they're dusty.  She turns off the vacuum cleaner and goes to the kitchen for the bottle of glass cleaner and a paper towel, but only a single paper towel remains.  She goes for a new roll of paper towels and finds the linen closet could use some straightening, which reminds her to switch the bathroom towels.  And she's off to the bathroom…"

But not even Bertie Higgins, overwhelmed by the tragedy of the bakery fire, could explain the steps taken as she straightened her home in anticipation of the Bellapanis.

At 3:00 A.M., hearing neither ring nor knock, a bottle of Windex in one hand and a dustpan in the other, Bertie walked to her front door.  She set the bottle and dustpan in the hallway and opened the door.  Mary Bellapani stood on the sidewalk staring blankly at Bertie from the bottom stair, holding fast to a clothes hamper.

Bertie held the lapels of her robe together against the chill, and seeing this, Mary seemed to realize how cold it was that November morning. A shiver began deep within her, shaking the vacuity from her stare.

"Petey and Joe?" Bertie asked.

"They're coming," Mary said, and Bertie felt Mary shudder from the cold, or from the fire. She walked down the steps.

A summer nightgown and the hamper were all that protected Mary against the cold, and when Bertie Higgins took the wicker vessel from her arms—surprised at the heft of it—and set it on the sidewalk, Mary's shiver rose to the surface. Her back teeth clicked with the cold, and her body trembled. Bertie untied her robe, and held it open for Mary, wrapping it around her friend as though it were meant for two people. Mary closed her eyes, and much of what she felt, Bertie knew. Mary felt the comfort of the robe, and its warmth, wrapping around her shoulders and at the small of her back. She wondered at its tremendous span, it seemed to cover her completely. Mary Bellapani thought that Bertie might have been an angel, and she wondered at the minor miracle of the robe that seemed to have grown in that instant to accommodate one of His least ones.

Mary pressed her cheek against Bertie's shoulder, and above her shivering breasts, barely covered by the thin threads of her summer nightgown, she felt the immediate warmth and substance of Bertie's own thinly veiled breasts. Instantly, Mary Bellapani was crying. She set forth a convulsion of sounds and tears, gasping and gulping at the November night to feed the release. It seemed to her that there could be no end to this great sobbing, that forever she would harbor the sorrow of this fire. On and on she sobbed.

Afraid to shut her eyes for fear she'd see more with them closed, for fear she'd know all that Mary had seen upon waking in her smoke and flame-filled place, Bertie looked at the fire. Over Mary's shoulder, smoke poured from the windows of the bakery in black pillowy clouds, and snaketongues of flame darted through the smoke. When she could take the sight no longer, Bertie looked down at the sidewalk, only to be saddened at seeing Mary's hamper—token for her, not of the things it contained, but of the things it did not.

Inside Bertie's robe, Mary's body trembled wildly, but even through the great expulsion of emotion, Bertie Higgins knew it would end. She could feel a tiny subsiding in the tremblings of Mary's breasts, and in the sounds of her wailing cry. She said nothing. She held Mary's face to her shoulder, and felt the warmth and wet of her tears, and knew the sadness would pass.

Bertie wished she had a power over fire then; she wished she could wave her hand or blow gently in the direction of the smoke and fire, and watch it disappear, or be sucked back in time. Better yet, she wished she could have prevented the fire in the first place. *That* would have been a gift. Immediately though, Bertie felt wrong for the wishing, for even Jesus couldn't stop fire. But in the presence of Mary's pain, all Bertie could do was wish for some power she didn't have. She could give Mary and her family a place to stay, but that was it. She could not wave her hands, or twinkle her nose, or click her heels and make fire disappear, nor could she keep Mary from the waking memory of fire, or the nightmares it was certain to urge. And because she held the edges of the robe at the small of Mary's back, it was a struggle for Bertie merely to lift her hands in order to shade Mary's face from the sight of the fire.

After some trouble though, she managed this meager service. With her right hand she held together the hemmed folds of her robe at Mary's back, and with her left, she tried to shade Mary's eyes from the flashes of fire. But Bertie could do nothing to screen the lambent dance of the fire from the side of Mary's face, each fugitive outburst of unshadeable light a reminder to Bertie of the roar and the raging heat of the flames Mary had just escaped.

Minutes passed before Bertie grew mindful of the softening

sadness of her friend. Mary's shuddering subsided, and soon her gasping demands for air lessened to sudden breaths, and then to whimpers, and then to the sighs of a fading cry, before disappearing altogether. And against the weight and warmth of her own nipples, Bertie felt the ever gentle softening of Mary's, felt each infinitesimal calibration from hard to soft; like the sluggish tickings of the tiniest second hand, she felt the softening of Mary. And Bertie forgot all of the things she was powerless to do: she could not stop fire or protect Mary from the memory of it; she could not replace furniture or appliances or turn back time in order to upgrade faulty electrical wiring. She could barely shade Mary's eyes from the fluttering play of the fire's light. But pressed against her, Bertie knew the miracle of breasts, the gift of them, and she believed, and felt blameless in believing, that it might have served Jesus well to have had breasts like hers.

When Mary pulled herself from Bertie's shoulder, she wiped her face with a section of the robe, and they ambled, as one, to the front door, passing the wicker hamper where Bertie had set it.

"Edward will bring it in," Bertie said.

As she ascended the stairs with her friend, Bertie felt as though the right thing to do would be to apologize for having a home, for at that moment, it seemed that it was evidence of a vulgar fortune. She was sidetracked at the top of the stairs, though, when Mary turned back to look at the steps they'd just climbed, eyeing them curiously, as though she could not recall having touched them. Halfway down the block, three figures were walking toward the Higgins's home from the direction of the bakery—three pairs of eyes locked on the swollen and somber hamper before them. Three fingers flicking at Bertie's heart.

This is a hamper in front of my house, is what Mr. Higgins was thinking. My friend Joe Bellapani and his family will be guests in my house.

This is all that is left, is what Joe Bellapani was thinking.

That's our hamper, is what Petey was thinking.  In the middle of a sidewalk.

The rest of Sunday passed in a fog.  There were three meals at the Higgins's house, each of them taken in an unbroken silence.  Several times, Sharon Higgins looked at Petey as he shifted his food on his plate with his fork.  She had wanted to say something, but there was no good thing to say.

When Petey Bellapani awoke on the Monday after the bakery fire, Mrs. Higgins was finger-combing his hair.  He flinched, and then she flinched, and when Petey started to speak his words caught in his throat.  He hadn't spoken in more than a day.

He cleared his throat.  "Where's my mother?" he tried again.

"She just now fell asleep, Petey.  She was up all night."

Through the half-open door of Petey's room, Sharon Higgins walked by.  The tallest girl in the seventh grade, she was tiptoeing toward the bathroom wearing only panties, and a T- shirt that left her midriff bare.  Just past the open doorway of the guest room, she stopped in her tracks, and sucked in the air through her clenched teeth, but it was too late to drag back her half-naked mistake.

Mrs. Higgins is touching my hair, Petey thought, and Sharon Higgins just walked past in her underwear.  I have school today.

He had hoped, even as he was half-pulled, half-carried from the burning apartment, that he might not have to go to school on Monday, but it seemed a bakery fire was not tragedy enough for that.  Petey looked down at his T-shirt and pajama bottoms.

"Do I have a uniform for school, Mrs. Higgins?"

This fact struck him then: the hamper on the sidewalk.  In the midst of the fire his mother had rescued the hamper.

It was true.  Though she hadn't held up so well since the fire, in the thick of panic and smoke, Mrs. Bellapani had proved surprisingly capable.  As flames darted along the walls of the apartment, she hadn't forfeited an ounce of her fair-weather composure. In the chaos of the heat and smoke and flames, she'd unveiled a logic that bordered on a kind of genius. Mary Bellapani had grabbed these things, in this order from the apartment above Dressel's Bakery: from the top of her dresser, her jewelry box; from her bedroom closet, a yellow dress she had never worn; from a cabinet in the dining room, a framed photograph of herself as a child; from a drawer of the buffet table in the living room, an accordion file of various papers, some official, some sentimental; and from the front closet, three pairs of shoes. Her final destination was the bathroom, and when she reached it, she opened the lid of the hamper and stuffed the things she'd gathered into it until its wicker sides creaked with the pressure.

Weeks later, Mr. Bellapani would ask his wife how she'd thought to salvage those things, but Mary would not recall her rationale. "The hamper is all I remember," she said. "I knew we'd never return. We would need clothes." And rather than go through three dressers in two rooms to see that everyone had at least a change of clothes, she'd opted for the democracy of the family hamper, knowing it contained a week's worth of clothing for each of them.

Bertie's face twisted apologetically when Petey asked her if he had a school uniform. Amid the haste to make sense of what remained, no one had laundered the clothes so sensibly rescued from the fire.

Mary Bellapani could hardly be blamed; for starters, she wasn't even in her own house, nor was she in any condition to attend to such details after such a tragedy. No, Bertie accepted full responsibility for the oversight.

It had been her intention to wash clothes for the Bellapanis. It was Sunday afternoon when she considered telling Mrs. Bellapani she'd be happy to do laundry for her, but she was afraid the question would only remind Mary of her loss, she seemed so fragile. Instead, Bertie recalled the hamper in the front hallway and took it upon herself to launder its contents.

When she lifted the lid, though, she discovered the shoes, a yellow dress, and a jewelry box. She poked aside several shoes until the edge of a framed photograph was revealed, and an accordion file, whereupon Bertie began to imagine Mary in the burning midst of a life she had grown and nurtured, frantically running through the apartment, snatching at items. Bertie found herself crying then, a thing that tended to sneak up on her, and when her vision finally cleared, the first thing that revealed itself to her was a clump of dust poking from under the couch in the living room. It would be hours before she attended to that clump, for several other projects: a cluttered pantry, a sprinkle of flour on the kitchen floor, and the absence of bread, milk, and pure vanilla—revealed themselves on her way to the closet where the broom was stored. And lost, of course, in the untraceable sequence of these revelations, was Bertie's intention to wash and dry clothes for the Bellapanis. Until Monday, that is.

"I'll see what I can do about a uniform, Petey," Mrs. Higgins said. She mumbled mild reproaches to herself as she walked to the hallway to re-explore the hamper, a week's worth of clothes crammed at the bottom. "Bertie Higgins," she said, "You were this close to the hamper yesterday." She pressed her finger and thumb together. "If you had just looked below the surface you would have seen the laundry. There could have been a basketful of clean clothes for everyone this morning." She imagined three neat piles of tightly folded clothes, one for each of the Bellapanis.

Petey's white school shirts, which Bertie pulled from the bottom of the hamper, were both stained—one with Sloppy Joe sauce on the pocket, the other with a spot of blood at the elbow, the size of a quarter. There may have been time to wash the clothes before school, but there was certainly none to dry them, so Bertie Higgins examined a White Sox T-shirt she found clumped in the hamper, and while she ironed it she considered writing a note for Petey's teacher to explain why he wouldn't be properly dressed. When she returned to him with the note, he looked at the tightly folded T-shirt in his hands.

"What about pants, Mrs. Higgins?"

And instead of crying when she looked into Petey's eyes, she hooked a fugitive wave of his hair around his ear and said, "Oh my, yes. You'll certainly be needing pants today."

She ironed his brown school pants straight from the hamper, and as it was with his T-shirt, though the wrinkles disappeared upon the ironing, and the smell of wicker and soiled clothes could only be faintly detected, the smell of fire was not so easily erased. Mrs. Higgins blasted them with Niagara spray starch, and glided the iron, steaming and hissing, over the pants. She pictured Petey sitting at his desk at St. David's, wearing his White Sox T-shirt, amid twenty-six uniformed boys and girls. Bertie stood still until the flicking at her heart passed.

Petey dressed while Bertie looked around for a sweater or jacket that he would agree to wear. Sharon waited by the open door until Petey joined her there. Seconds later, Mrs. Higgins came to the door holding two of Sharon's jackets.

"I'll be fine like this, Mrs. Higgins," he said.

"Are you sure?" she asked.

"It's not so cold out, Mom," Sharon said. "He'll be fine."

Through all but a few steps of their walk to school, neither Petey nor Sharon said a word. For an entire block, Petey kicked his way through the fallen leaves on the patches of grass along the curb. On the next block he avoided the leaves entirely, tiptoeing between them on the gray spaces of cement. He reached out to catch a leaf as it fell from a maple tree, but it eluded him. On the next block he stepped right foot first over every crack in the sidewalk.

Sharon had known Petey since kindergarten, and from the moment she woke up on Sunday morning and learned what had happened to his apartment, she had wanted to say something to him. She'd promised herself that before they got to school, she'd say it, whatever it was, because she knew that as soon as they arrived, it would be too late. Petey would join the boys, and she'd join the girls, and it would be as if they had not even known each other.

She looked his way a couple of times and watched him nudge his shoulder to his nose, sniffing the sleeve of his T-shirt. He picked up a thorny half-shell of a horse chestnut when they reached Union Avenue and clipped the thorns off with his thumbnail as they walked, which was when Sharon noticed Petey didn't have any of his school things. Her own books, neatly protected with paper-bag jackets, labeled along the bindings, stood on their ends in the canvas shoulder bag her mother had made for her.

As they approached Emerald Avenue, Mrs. Pell started walking to their side of the street. It seemed to Sharon that the crossing guard had been watching Petey since the middle of the block, and she decided she had to speak to Petey before Mrs. Pell did.

She would tell Petey that she was sorry about the fire, and that they were going to eat dinner together tonight, like a family, and there would be pork chops with crispy fried onions, and mashed potatoes, and broccoli tonight, and she'd tell him that she'd walk home with him after school if he wanted to, and that it felt kind of like they were living together in a way. And maybe there would be kids who would tease them because Petey was living at her house. But even if they did, Sharon would tell him that she didn't care; she was glad that Petey had a place to stay and she was glad it was at her house. She'd even tell Petey that she knew he saw her pass by his room this morning wearing only a T-shirt and underwear and even that didn't matter. And she felt that everything would be ruined if Mrs. Pell spoke before Sharon.

"Petey?" she finally said, and she looked at him. The horse chestnut was a smooth ball of green in his hands.

"Yeah?" he said.

"If you want to, we could share books today," Sharon said. Petey waited a few seconds to reply. He clenched his teeth, and it seemed to Sharon as though he was about to cry, and she wanted to hug him, she didn't care if she didn't say anything else.

"OK," he said.

"And for homework tonight, too," Sharon said. "If you want to."

Across the street, the school playground was filling with students, and Petey wished that the school day had already ended and he were walking home, walking to the Higgins's house with Sharon. They would sit at the dining room table and do their homework together, and if he got stuck on a problem she could help him with it, and maybe he'd talk to her about the fire.

"OK," Petey said.

Mrs. Pell said nothing. She walked Sharon and Petey across Emerald Avenue, touching Petey's shoulder as she guided him across, and Sharon felt that she'd told Petey Bellapani all there was to say.

Petey had not expected anything like the welcome he received when he arrived at school that morning. As he crossed Emerald Avenue, the last street before St. David's, most of the boys in his class had already gathered in the school playground. They formed a tight circle of brown pants and white shirts with brown plaid ties near the strike zone painted on the brick wall of the rectory garage. The plaid-skirted girls assembled at the swing set near the faculty parking lot. Each of them wore dark brown sweaters over their collared shirts. Ella Bedore was sitting on the swing, but it wasn't moving.

Sharon looked at Petey before they walked to their respective circles. "See you later, Petey," she said.

"OK," he said.

As Sharon walked toward her classmates, Ella Bedore stood up from the swing and held the chain aside for Sharon to take her place, as though the act had been agreed upon ahead of time. Sharon suggested, with a gesture and a whispered sound, that they say nothing to Petey about the fire or about his clothes or anything, and all seemed to agree, by way of their own secret gestures, that this was sensible. As the girls murmured quietly and looked over their shoulders toward Petey, it felt to Sharon as if they were all sisters.

Petey walked slowly toward the boys, and Billy Paresi, who lived down the street from Dressel's, stood at the nave of the huddle. Petey had little doubt that Billy was telling everyone about the fire, and when Chris Wagner turned his head away from the huddle and noticed Petey coming, Petey felt it was just like Paresi to benefit from someone else's fire.

All of them turned their heads toward Petey then, and Petey stopped walking. He stood by the lone tree in the playground, a maple that grew from a square of dirt framed with cedar logs. Ronny "The Goat" Frugoli was the first to step toward Petey. Davy Stewart stepped ahead of The Goat quickly, but The Goat held his arm out stiffly and Davy slowed down. Every boy in the seventh grade walked slowly toward Petey, then. In the middle of the group, Billy Paresi was looking right into Petey's eyes, and against the secret thrill of the procession that came toward him, Petey no longer cared that Billy had stolen his story.

It was a struggle to breathe, but Petey felt like smiling, too. Every boy knew what it meant to be a hero. You needed only to have a thing that other boys wanted—a pocketknife, a cut that needed stitches, parents who let your friends sit on your porch or play cards in your basement—and you were a hero. But even as he considered the word *hero* as a possibility for the thing he felt, he knew that *this* was different. He recalled his father on the night of the fire, fleeing the hallway of the bakery building, holding tight to the statue of the Pilgrim Virgin. Together they'd watched the flames from across the street until there was nothing left for his father to protect. And since the fire, Petey's mother had cried all weekend. She was probably crying right now. This heroism came with a burden, with a fist clenching in his stomach, and Petey wanted the boys to know just how different this really was. This was not a heroism you could be proud of. This was not like having a patch on your eye, or a plaster cast on your broken arm.

And in those few seconds it took for them to walk toward him, Petey weighed the burden against the thrill, the heaviness of the one and the lightness of the other, and not until Davy Stewart, the first boy to reach him, spoke, was Petey able to detach himself from the heavier thing.

"My mom said you could've died," Davy said, and all the boys stopped in their tracks, waiting for someone else to speak. But it was Davy who spoke again.

"She said your whole family could've died in the fire."

It was true, Petey thought, Davy's mother had said something true. A bakery and sixteen apartments had burned to the ground, nearly everything was lost, but Petey and his family had escaped with their lives. Petey—who could have been dead—stood now in the middle of a circle of boys, very much alive. He could not take credit, of course, for having saved his family from certain death; *that* would have been something. But fire had surrounded him. It had crackled and raged along the walls of his home, shattering glass, and taking everything. But Petey was alive and had a story about fire, could tell the story of fire to boys now, if he cared to. He could tell how he stood in the middle of the living room, staring at his own bare feet and wondering where his shoes were. He could tell how Gus Valenti, a punk of local fame, a punk his father hated, had banged the door down and screamed, "Mary! Joe! Get up! Mr. Bellapani! Fire!" He could tell how Gus grabbed his arm and pulled him into the hallway, how they both flew down three flights, touching only four stairs. He could tell how the firemen seemed to move in slow motion in the smoke-filled stairwell, looking in his eyes and nodding at Gus Valenti, how one of them had winked at Petey. He could tell how, once they were outside, his father wanted him to walk to the Higginses' house with his mother, but Petey had stayed, watching the fire and the smoke. He could tell how, when he looked in the bathroom mirror at the Higginses' house, he found that soot had gathered at the corners of his mouth and nose and eyes. And how he twisted a square of toilet paper into his nostrils, and, when he pulled it out, it was black with smoke and ash.

But he couldn't find the words to tell the boys anything as they drew around him. He couldn't say a thing about the flames, or the heat, or the smoke, or the black ash in his nostrils, for the weight of the clenched fist he felt in his chest had softened and lifted itself to a place just behind his eyes, and despite the excitement of his newly acquired heroism, he was sure that if he spoke about the fire just then, he would cry.

A warm November breeze began to rustle above him. It started at the top of the maple tree they had gathered under, and as it blew through the body of the tree, it released a few of the leaves that still clung to the branches.

From where Sharon Higgins stood with the girls and tried not to watch, she saw a gold maple leaf, the size of a newborn baby's hand, settle onto Petey's shoulder. She remembered on their walk, how Petey had tried to catch a leaf but it had escaped his hand.

Petey remembered that, too, when he saw the spot of gold on his shoulder, and just then the smell of fire on his shirt returned to him. He thought the smell of fire was like a scar that would never leave. He would always smell it on his clothes and in his hair. It occurred to him that this smell had been added to his life. And Petey felt for a moment that a very bad trade had been executed without his consent: the smell of everything the Bellapanis had owned, for the smell of fire.

Petey picked the leaf from his shoulder and put it in his pocket. He would give it to Sharon later. And as the weight behind his eyes pushed forward and threatened to turn into tears, Petey said the only thing he could think to say to the boys who circled around him.

"Smell my shirt," he said. And he lifted a pinch of his shirt toward the boys, the "o" of "Sox" between his thumb and finger.

For a moment no one moved. Petey felt a single tear hold at the outside edge of his eye.

"It smells like fire," Petey said. Then Davy Stewart walked up to him and put his nose against Petey's shirt. He took a deep whiff of the fire. Then he looked into Petey's eyes and nodded. Next, Chris Wagner smelled Petey's shirt, followed by The Goat, and then Johnny Foglio and Johnny Dimon. And without talking, without the rush or push to which they were accustomed, the rest of the boys of the class of 1976 formed a line, and each of them leaned into Petey's shirt so that they might put a smell to what Petey had become.

# The Logic of a Rose

At the end of November the Bellapanis moved into a brick two-flat in the middle of Thirty-first and Wallace, a block and a half-world away from the charred remains of their apartment above Dressel's Bakery. There were no trees there, no bushes or front lawns, no flower boxes hanging from windowsills, no weeds making their way through cracks in the cement. There was nothing green anywhere.

Beneath the first-floor windows of the new house, though, two feet below the sidewalk, there was a rectangle of hard dirt the size of a coffin. A spiked, wrought iron fence protected the stretched square of earth from whatever humans might threaten such a place, but it did little to keep away lesser culprits; for the dirt garden, Mary Bellapani would soon learn, was the end of the journey for much of the litter of Wallace Avenue. Hot dog wrappers, lunch bags, empty match books, chewing gum foil, baseball card wrappers, newspaper pages, even pop bottles and beer cans found their way through the iron bars. Mary cleared the garbage the day they moved in, but by the next morning it had been replaced by the litter of another day.

Privately—which is to say, without telling a soul—Mary Bellapani cursed the litterbugs who threw garbage in her garden, but the criminals were not human. Geography and a crazy wind were the only scoundrels in cahoots against her. Vortices of wind formed there, calling the detritus of Bridgeport to the rectangle of dirt, where it swirled in tiny whirlwinds that swept the length of the space. Tin cans clinked against the concrete walls of the ugly garden.

Mrs. Bellapani vowed to fight against the ugliness there. She promised to spend the winter planning a complex and colorful garden, for she was certain it would discourage the degenerates responsible for the trash. She purchased seeds from a mail-order catalogue and set them in a box near the front door. She bought a trowel, yellow gardening gloves, and a watering can; and she planned to make something lovely grow the minute spring arrived.

But when a freak warm front came to Bridgeport in late November, Mrs. Bellapani felt it was a sign for her to step up her plans so she wouldn't have to wait. There would be flowers by spring. She settled on an array of tulip bulbs; she'd heard they could be planted as late as the first of December. They were hearty little things, she'd heard.

Petey turned the earth for her. He climbed over the railing and hopped into the garden. He speared the ground with a spade, but the dirt was hard—not so much from cold as neglect—and the tip of the shovel barely cut into the earth. He jumped on the feet of the spade to push the point deeper, and when that first shovelful went from gray to black, Mrs. Bellapani smiled. She watched Petey turn the rest of the garden, and when he finished, she started to climb carefully over the railing that edged the stairs. Petey held his hand out to assist her. She used a yardstick to space the bulbs evenly, planted three columns of tulips, fifteen across, and left the Chicago sky to provide what little water the bulbs would need to make it through winter. Petey hoped for the best, though he felt it was odd to plant flowers before winter. It seemed a lot to ask of tulips.

The first snow came, wet and heavy, one week into December; even as it fell it was gray, and before any sport could be made of it, a six-day blast of bitter cold froze it over. January followed, scratching and clawing and biting from beginning to end, when another snowstorm buried Bridgeport. Early February froze it over again. On Valentine's Day, the weather warmed enough to make a dirty mess of a winter's deposit of snow, and that's how it stayed. Piles of plowed and shoveled snow, black and hard, lined the curbs. Along Wallace Avenue and every street in Bridgeport, homeowners saved their shoveled parking spaces with lawn chairs, milk crates, and two-by-fours, but sometimes it was not enough. Sometimes punches had to be thrown to protect the hard-earned spaces.

It wasn't the kind of winter children played in. It wasn't pure and playful like grown-ups remember their childhood winters. If the lifeless and icy air didn't sting you with pain, there was a wet freeze you couldn't shake. It chilled you so deep you felt the wet of it in your bones, so that even when you went inside and sat against the radiator for an hour you couldn't shake it. There was reason to believe that spring would never come.

But the Bellapanis made the most of it. Against the weight of the bakery fire that had burned everything, a Chicago winter didn't seem so bad. They made a new home for themselves. They scoured shelves, and lined them with new contact paper. They pulled the oven away from the wall and bleached away the years of dust and crumbs and grease collected there, they replaced the cabinet hardware in the kitchen, they scrubbed floors, scraped wallpaper, and painted floors.

They worked. Petey delivered the *Tribune* and *Sun-Times* out of the Wallace Newspaper Office, and bought his own clothes with his tips. Joe Bellapani picked up a second job, delivering for Connie's Pizza.

Mary Bellapani worked the breakfast shift at Papa John's on Princeton Avenue. It was the first time since her teens that she had a paying job, and each week, she kept aside some of her tips. When she had enough money saved, she bought a stereo system to replace the hi-fi that had burned in the fire. She had money left over for two Billy Joel albums.

Mr. Bellapani said he thought the stereo should go in the dining room, but Mary didn't think so; when she closed her eyes she could see the summertime, she could see herself sitting on the porch on a summer afternoon with a glass of lemonade in her hand, the shade of the house moving across the street, ice cubes clinking in her glass. She could hear the bottom of the glass scrape on the gritty cement of the front porch, could see the circle of perspiration it made. And she could imagine music on a summer afternoon, with the front window open and the curtains billowing, so the stereo went in the front room.

In March, the Calabrese family moved into the upstairs flat. There were Mr. and Mrs. Calabrese, who didn't speak a word of English. They were tiny. Dark and serious. There was Gina, who was two years older than Petey, a sophomore at St. Mary of Perpetual Help, and there was Rosalie, Petey's age, who went to St. Anthony's on Twenty-sixth Street.

Sometimes Petey would see Mr. and Mrs. Calabrese walking home from the grocery store, or talking to Mr. Bellapani on the front porch, but no one saw much of Gina or Rosalie that first month on account of the nasty winter that clung to March.

On a Saturday that month, while Petey lunched on a grilled cheese sandwich and a bowl of tomato soup, he asked his mother about Rosalie.

"Does the girl upstairs speak English?"

"There are *two* girls who live upstairs, Petey," she said, and looked at Petey as though he were asking something else altogether.

"The younger one," Petey said.

"Rosalie," his mother said. "Yes. Her sister also speaks English."

"You know, Petey," she continued, "why don't you go upstairs and ask Rosalie if she'd like to come down for some hot Bosco. She's the same age as you."

It was not the first time Petey's mother had mentioned the coincidence of her age. Petey understood there was something about the age of things that mattered. No one considered suggesting Petey have Bosco with Gina, for instance, the difference between twelve and fourteen mattering a great deal.

Late that March, as he walked toward his house from Thirty-second Street, Petey saw Rosalie standing in the open crack of her front door, leaning toward the Bellapanis' flat, wearing a black sweater, her arms folded against the cold. She hadn't seen Petey coming, and when he said, "Hi," she flinched, slammed the door, and ran up the stairs. Petey listened to her slippered feet slap against the wooden steps. She seemed like a secret.

Upstairs, Rosalie's heart pounded against her skin so hard she pressed her hand against it to keep it in.

As Petey walked to his front door that afternoon, he heard music blaring from the stereo in the living room. In the kitchen, his mother was on her hands and knees washing the floor, singing along with Billy Joel. Rosalie was listening to the music, Petey thought. That's why she was standing there in her doorway, and why she looked as though she'd been caught doing something wrong when she saw him coming. Maybe she couldn't listen to American music in her own house. Maybe her parents only let her listen to Italian music.

And because it was still winter, and there was nothing better to do, or perhaps because Rosalie was twelve years old, Petey began playing the records, too. By then, Mrs. Bellapani's collection had grown, but Petey stuck to Billy Joel. As long as his father wasn't home yet, he'd turn the volume up high and open the window a crack so that Rosalie might better hear the music. He never checked to see if she was listening; he was afraid he might scare her away. Instead, he would bring one of the dining room chairs into the hallway and listen from there, he'd lean back in the chair against the wall and try not to sing along in anything more than a whisper, but sometimes he'd catch himself singing louder than he meant to. He'd imagine Rosalie just inches away from him, standing in her doorway, her arms folded, listening for Petey's voice as he sang. Petey listened for the squeak of her door opening, for the creaking of floorboards in her hallway.

April came as it always did in Bridgeport, with only a hint that it was spring. You could count on April for wet and cold, and maybe a day or two of a bit of sun and mild temperatures, but only dreamers and passers-through were ever fooled into hope by fair April days. If you put any stock in a decent day, you'd get your heart broken so fast your head would spin. April didn't have a heart, it had balls. It didn't show off for new people in town. If you lived in Chicago long enough, you knew that, you knew what you were getting with April: with any luck the snow would melt. You couldn't hope for much more than that.

All winter long, Mrs. Bellapani had Petey shovel the snow from the sidewalk into the tulip garden so that it would feed the tulip bulbs when it melted. In April, though, the snow he'd piled there was black and ugly. It was the last snow in the neighborhood to disappear, and as it melted it dragged a black stain against the house.

When the snow finally cleared, Petey looked in on the dirt garden after his paper route each morning. If garbage had appeared through the night, he'd sneak into the space and remove it before his mother awoke, so that as she started toward Papa John's each day, she would be glad to see she was winning her fight against litter. As for the tulips, Petey wondered at the reluctance of the nubs to break ground; April was nearly over and the tulips had yet to appear.

But even in Chicago, April summoned May. And May had a heart. It was small and sometimes hard to see, but it was a heart, and on his way back from his paper route, when he wheeled his wagon into the orange ball of sun rising from the east end of Thirty-first Street, Petey felt the hope and throb of it.

He met Rosalie on the first of May, the day he helped his father and Mr. Calabrese take the storm windows down. The weather was still cool, and it was a school night, but it was Mr. Bellapani's first spring as a homeowner, and several times, he'd said he refused to allow the storm windows to stay up in May. He and Mr. Calabrese spoke in Italian while they worked. It was

full and round. Sentences started slow and soft and then rolled
and waved like music. It sped and danced and grew so loud that
Petey was sure his father and Mr. Calabrese were yelling at each
other, but when Petey looked at their faces to see if they were
mad, they would laugh or smile, and the volume would fade to
soft for a while. Around and around it went. Petey knew a few
Italian words, but he had no idea what the two of them spoke
about that day.

When they took the last storm window down, Mrs.
Calabrese came to the front porch. In her presence, Petey
thought he noticed something happen in the men, as if seeing
her there reminded them of something. They seemed pleased
with themselves. They stood, Petey thought, like soldiers after
a shift.

Petey leaned the last of the windows against the iron railing
at the bottom stair. He heard the word *biscotti* as Mrs. Calabrese
spoke to the men. That word he knew. Cookies were on their
way.

"*Si. Si. Va bene. Grazie,*" Mr. Bellapani said, and turned
toward Petey.

"Go get your mother," he said. "Mrs. Calabrese is coming
down with Bosco and cookies."

Through the ceiling came the mumbled sounds of Italian
girls fussing to feed men, and in that moment Petey felt like a
soldier himself. He rushed his invitation to his mother to join
them for cookies and then returned to the porch. There was
movement on the stairway, the sound of the six slippered feet of
Mrs. Calabrese and her daughters tapping on the stairs. It was
the sound of light and hope; it was the sound of May.

Mrs. Calabrese and Gina each held trays of steaming cups
of Bosco. Rosalie carried a tray of cookies. She smiled and
lowered her eyes as she directed the tray, first to Petey's father,
and then his mother. Next, she walked to Petey, and as she
held the biscotti before him, she looked up. He wondered if
she even knew his name. He was going to say, "Hi, my name
is Petey," but she had lived upstairs for two months, and he felt

like she should already have known his name, even though
they'd never really met. In a way, it seemed he had already been
in communication with her. And as Petey Bellapani prepared
to meet Rosalie Calabrese's gaze, he wanted to say hello. He
wanted to say his name so that she knew, for a fact, what it was,
and maybe she'd use it some day.

Rosalie raised her eyes to him. Petey felt he'd been waiting
for that moment for months, but she pulled her head away so
quickly he thought he'd made the mistake of saying too much,
though he hadn't said a word—not with his voice anyway. He
wondered if he'd looked too closely in her eyes, though, if he'd
somehow told her with his eyes that it was he all along who'd
been playing the music, and that he'd been playing it for her.
And maybe now she knew. Maybe she'd been listening to it
every day from the open crack of her front door, and sometimes
she'd even heard him singing and now maybe she was afraid
that if she looked in Petey's eyes too long he'd know everything,
too, and so would everyone else, and that's why she looked
away so quickly.

However briefly she'd looked at him, though, it was long
enough for Petey to see her eyes. They were the color of the
cracked green olives from Dressel's Bakery. And the thin black
lines that spread like spokes from their black centers were so
dark it seemed as though someone had painted them with the
skinniest of paintbrushes and the steadiest of hands. Petey
wondered if there were paintbrushes skinny enough to paint
such lines. He wondered if she had to lower her eyes because of
the effect they might have on people, or maybe she knew they
were so beautiful that people would be sad to see them. Or
maybe she thought she didn't deserve her eyes, they were too
beautiful for someone to have.

By the time Petey accepted a cookie from her, Rosalie
had lowered her head. She turned away and held the tray of
biscotti toward Mr. Calabrese. Petey thought he might know,
as he looked at the side of her face, how she'd look when she was
old, and he wondered if she could tell the same thing when she

looked at him. He wished, for a moment, that he could be her father or her mother, so that he could see her eyes again.

And so the Bellapanis and the Calabreses ate cookies and clinked their cups. Mr. Bellapani made a toast to the Calabreses, and Mr. Calabrese made a toast to the Bellapanis. They toasted the house and Chicago, and Mr. Calabrese made a toast to America. It sounded like a different place when he said *America*, but Petey counted it as the first word of English he'd ever heard Rosalie's father say. Mr. Calabrese's eyes looked soft when he said America, and Petey wondered if he had meant to toast Italy instead.

When Rosalie tapped her cup against Petey's, she looked at him again for a second. Petey looked closely. He wanted to see if her eyes were really the color of olives, if there were thin black lines painted through them like spokes.

Rosalie smiled, which made Petey look at her mouth, and he felt he'd been fooled, that she'd smiled at him to call him away from her eyes. And it felt like the official start of a new life, a kind of grand opening. April was gone, and the possibility of a freak snow and cold were gone as well, and Petey had met Rosalie. Her eyes were green and it was May.

The next day arrived with enough warmth and promise to convince the hardest of hearts that winter had spent itself. Mr. Bellapani walked with a swagger, as though he were responsible for how nice the day was, it being his idea to take down the storm windows the day before. It was a Friday, and all through school Petey felt as though it were a summer day. At lunchtime, Davy Stewart and The Goat told Petey he should hang out with them that night at Bernie's, the corner store on Thirty-second and Wallace.

"Mikey Rico, Paully Bertucci, Eddie Parelli and those guys hang out there," Davy said.

The guys on the corner were fifteen and sixteen, most of them, but they didn't seem to mind Davy and The Goat hanging out with them, even though they were only thirteen. They were big for their age, especially The Goat. He played softball on a men's team at McGuane Park, the same team as Billy B., his cousin, who also hung out on the corner. The Goat's real name was Ronny, but one day he started telling everyone to call him The Goat, which stood for the Greatest of all Time, so that's what everyone called him. The Goat told Petey they'd stop by his house after dinner to get him on their way to the corner.

After school that day, Petey noticed columns of tiny green tulip nubs poking their way through the dirt garden. He told his mother this as he changed into his play clothes.

"Well, I'll be," she said. She walked to the front door to look at them. "You were only waiting for May, weren't you?" she asked the tulips.

Petey was racing through the living room as his mother was heading back in.

"Whoa," she said. "Where're you going?"

"I don't know," he said. "Just out."

"Slow down, Petey," she said. "Whatever it is, it'll wait for you."

Petey jumped down the stairs and had taken two strides toward Thirty-first Street before he saw Rosalie from the corner of his eye. He stopped and turned back toward the porch.

"Hi," he said.

"Hi," Rosalie said. In perfect English.

"Did you see the tulips?" he asked.

"Yes," she said. "I saw them yesterday."

"While we were on the porch?" Petey asked. He wanted to be sure that yesterday had happened, and that Rosalie remembered it.

"Yes."

Petey leaned against the railing and looked up at Rosalie. She wore her skirt from St. Anthony's, and on her navy blue sweater there was a cross and shield. When she looked back at him, he was surprised again by her eyes.

"It's like a summer day," he said.

Rosalie said nothing.

"In school, after lunch, I kept looking at the clock," Petey said, "thinking the bell would never ring."

"I know," Rosalie said.

"Aren't you hot in that sweater?" Petey said.

"No," she said.

"*Rosalie!*"

Mrs. Calabrese's call came from the door at the top of the stairway. Rosalie said goodbye with a flick of her wrist. She rushed up the stairs and was gone.

Petey stayed on the porch after Rosalie left. Against the possibility of her return, there was nothing better to do. At the north end of the stairs he looked into the tulip garden, and counted forty-five tulips; some had barely nudged their way through the gray crust and into the air.

She was pretty, Petey thought as he looked at the tulip nubs, but in a way that Davy and The Goat might not be able to see, or maybe wouldn't understand. She was like a girl you'd meet on vacation, dark and Italian and skinny and quiet, a girl from another place.

That spring would be the only time the front garden would grow according to a plan. Tulips would sprout again, but only erratically, in clumps that migrated from year to year. Nothing else would grow there, no matter what Mrs. Bellapani planted. Sickened by the hearty and disobedient bulbs, she would tear them out one summer, only to see them return the next spring in some new disorder. But today, now that Petey had spoken with Rosalie, the rectangle of earth could properly be called a tulip garden.

By the time Davy and The Goat had come to the corner with Petey, Ray Ray and Robby Pecca were already there. Billy B., The Goat's cousin, was there, too. They were pitching nickels.

"Wait here, Petey." The Goat pointed at the sidewalk short of Bernie's, and then walked up to Billy B. with Davy. Over their shoulders Billy looked at Petey and nodded, and then The Goat and Davy returned to where Petey stood.

"It's cool," he said, and they all joined the group on the corner. Davy and The Goat pitched nickels with the older guys while Petey sat on the ledge outside Bernie's and watched. He reminded himself to bring nickels next time.

There were girls there, too. Rita Bova and Jody Cosentino sat in the doorway of Penny's, the candy store that was never open, and anytime a car sped past, they both looked up to see who was in it. Debbie Vaccaro was there, too; she was with Mikey Rico. Mikey was leaning against the brick wall between two windows and Debbie had her hips pressed against him. He was smoking a Kool cigarette, and after he dragged on it, the smoke still in his mouth, Debbie kissed him on the lips. It was the longest kiss Petey had ever seen, and he couldn't help but watch, and when Debbie finally pulled away, she blew out the smoke from Mikey's cigarette into the sky and laughed. Then she looked at Petey and winked at him.

People came and went all night long. Cars passed and beeped horns. Sometimes cars pulled up to the curb and a passenger, riding shotgun, waved one of the guys over and they talked through the open window. Petey tried not to stare at Debbie Vaccaro, but it wasn't easy.

Petey left the corner at nine o'clock. The Goat told him they'd be there on Friday and Saturday, and Billy B. said it would be all right if Petey came again.

A string of beautiful spring days followed, and even people like the Bellapanis, who knew only Chicago weather—how it could break your heart if you looked the other way—were dazzled. The days were like a crush. They mashed you, they fooled you, made you say you'd never leave the place, not even for a minute.

Petey saw Rosalie on the porch again, after school the next day. She said hello, but not much more. She sat on the top stair against her door and Petey sat on a lower stair with his back against the railing. Petey wanted to hear about Italy, but was afraid to ask Rosalie too many questions, for fear she'd go upstairs, so he told her about his friends. He told her about the fire above the bakery.

They met again the next day, and there was more to talk about. He talked about St. David's and how mean the teachers were. He told her about Sister Agatha, who stepped on your toes if you got a math problem wrong, and Sister Hildegard, who whacked your hand with a ruler if your fingernails were too long. Rosalie told Petey that her parents were thinking of opening a hotdog stand where Penny's was. Every day they met on the porch after school. Rosalie sat against her door, and Petey leaned against the railing or stood on the sidewalk, bouncing a rubber ball against the stairs. Rarely were they there very long, though, before someone screamed Rosalie's name from upstairs, and she'd say 'Bye,' in the quickest way and then she'd be gone. One day a motorcycle roared down Wallace, and Petey turned around to watch it pass, and by the time he looked up Rosalie was gone.

And May summoned June.

When school finally ended for the summer, the Hotdog Hallway opened, as Rosalie said it would. Gina and Mrs. Calabrese did most of the work at first. Sometimes Mr. Calabrese was there on the weekends, and Rosalie filled in once in a while, but mostly she kept things together at home. It meant that sometimes she could sit on the porch without someone screaming her name from upstairs.

It took one full week of a school-free summer for Petey Bellapani to remember that there had ever been such a place as the Wallace Playlot. By then it was the ninth of June, and there was nothing to suggest that anything but brick houses had ever stood on the northeast corner of Thirty-third and Wallace Streets. The yellow dirt softball field, in which entire boyhoods had been lived, was gone, had disappeared without argument or trace.

Until then, no one seemed to realize what the playlot had meant to hundreds of boys, through hundreds of boyhoods. If their schools or their churches had been taken away, mothers and fathers would have been up in arms. They would have asked how could such things be taken away. But mothers and fathers weren't aware of what the playlot had been—their sons played softball there, is what they thought. It was a place for boys to be without them.

And though softball was what they did there most often, catching and hitting were the least of the things they learned. They learned everything else that you couldn't acquire at school: how to play against other boys, how to fight against them to win, and how to play with them afterward. It was where boys learned how to make mistakes and how to forgive them.

Because there were no grownups around, though, none of this was recorded, and when some unseen group of men decided that better use could be made of the real estate, there were no protests, and with the playlot went things to do, went promise held by summer.

For Petey, the mornings weren't so bad. In the mornings there was Rosalie. They'd sit on the porch and listen to Mrs. Bellapani's albums and talk, and like clockwork, at the stroke of eleven, Rosalie raced up the stairs to scrub and clean what must have been a spotless place, for all the time she spent tending it. But then the midday heat came down on Bridgeport like a punishment. The afternoons were hot and slow and long, and the sun hung in the sky like a thing to hate. It scorched and burned. It made dust, and beat on empty streets.

Petey practiced pitching nickels on the cement in front of the Med Center. He bought bottles of pop and sat on the ledge outside Bernie's, spitting puddles on the sidewalk between his feet, and looking for familiar faces in the cars that passed. Sometimes Robby Pecca came by with Ray Ray and smoked cigarettes, flicking their butts into the street, and there was no good place to hide from the sun.

Petey was sitting on the ledge outside Bernie's one day, when Mikey Rico nodded to him on his way inside. When he left the store, Mikey had a pack of Kool cigarettes and an RC Cola in his hands. He sat down, turning his pack of smokes upside down and banging it against the ledge between him and Petey.

Petey asked him what he was doing.

"Packing the tobacco," Mikey said. "It packs the tobacco tight up against the filter."

From the pocket of his T-shirt, Rico pulled out his old pack of Kools. He squinted in the square hole that had been peeled away from the pack. It was almost empty. He flicked his wrist and the last cigarette of the pack flipped up, and rolled to the curb. Petey stood to pick it up, but Mikey put his hand out to stop him.

"Fuck it, Petey. I ain't smokin' a cigarette that's been on the fuckin' curb. I got a fresh pack here."

Mikey opened the new pack and lit a cigarette. He put it between his thumb and forefinger, and he formed his other fingers into the sign of OK. Petey thought of how Debbie had kissed the smoke from Mikey's mouth that night in front of Bernie's.

When Rico left, Petey waited until he was out of sight, then picked the cigarette up from the curb and brought it back to the ledge. He laid it across the palm of his hand and closed his fingers around it. When he was sure no cars would pass, he held the cigarette between his thumb and forefinger and made the sign of OK. He sat there by himself, hidden from the world, waiting for something to happen.

Exactly how it happened, Petey couldn't be sure. But something came by the corner of Thirty-second and Wallace Streets when only boys, the last of the boys in Bridgeport were there. It swooped in like a villain in a big green Chevy, and slammed its brakes at the corner, squealing its tires and spraying open its doors. It jumped out with a baseball bat turned cudgel, and ransacked boyhood like it was a lemonade stand. It broke the legs of the table, smashing the pitcher of lemonade into a thousand shards of glass. It stole their money and punched them in the stomachs. And when the boys folded over and clutched at their bellies, it reached down and gripped its fingers into the hollows of their arms and pulled them to their feet. Putting its sinewy arms on their shoulders, it whispered to them like a compassionate friend. It had smoke and drink on its breath, and it flipped them each a cigarette and taught them how to inhale; told them a pack of smokes only cost sixty cents, and gave them a buck apiece from its own pocket to get them started. It introduced them to Mexican Mike who bought peppermint schnapps and blackberry brandy for them if they gave him some "chum change" for his trouble. And then the last boys in Bridgeport looked over their shoulders at the ghost of the Wallace Playlot, and prepared to spit on it one last time, to expel the last remnant of boyhood. But what came out of their mouths was not the spit of boys, not a misting stream of saliva sprayed from their front teeth, or a clean dot of foam, but with a grinding, throaty pull, somewhere between their lungs and the hot afternoon air, the innocent spit of boys became the first green hocker of growing up, and they thwacked it onto the place where a playlot had been. They left it there uncovered. Didn't even watch the last yellow dust of the playlot curl up at the hocker's rim.

Across the street from the Hotdog Hallway, the Bridgeport Medical Center and apartment building stood six floors tall, higher than any building in Bridgeport. Robby Pecca's aunt Kimmy lived on the fifth floor. She was only a few years older than Robby.

Robby told Petey one day that Kimmy used to baby-sit him and his little brother Joey. "She used to change her clothes right in front of us," Robby said. "She coulda gone in the bedroom or the bathroom and change, but she didn't. She comes into the room and we'd be watching TV, and she'd stand in front of the TV and she'd be over there, 'Close your eyes, Robby. Close your eyes, Joey. Don't peek. I gotta change my shirt.' And Joey would be over there closing his eyes," Robby said, "But I'd be over there, putting my hands over my eyes, looking at her titties through the spaces in my fingers."

By the time July of 1974 rolled through Bridgeport, though, Robby was too old for a baby-sitter, and Kimmy was selling dope out of her apartment. She bought pot by the quarter-pound, rolled it into joints, and sold them for a buck apiece, out of a tin of Sucrets lozenges. "Can you keep a sucret," she'd say, and then she'd laugh like it was the funniest thing she'd ever heard.

Petey and Robby were in Kimmy's apartment one afternoon, the weed nearly covering her coffee table. After they'd rolled all the dope into joints, Kimmy lit one and pulled a lungful of smoke from it. She passed it to Robby and he dragged from it and held the smoke in his lungs, sucking it deeper and deeper until he blew and no smoke came out.

Petey had been smoking cigarettes for three weeks, and just the day before, Rico had sold Petey a joint of marijuana stems for a dollar. Petey didn't know it was a joke, but everyone else did. He was alone in the alley behind the Redwood Lounge when he lit the end of the joint. He dragged the smoke and when he pulled it into his lungs it felt as though he'd sucked in fire. Petey hacked away until his throat was raw and his head throbbed.

Compared to the stems, though, the joint Petey smoked in Kimmy's apartment was nothing. He held the smoke in his lungs for a few seconds and then blew it out. A warm summer cloud filled his head, easy and sweet and light. One toke would have been enough, he thought, but most of the joint was gone by the time Robby asked Kimmy if he could take Petey up to the roof of the Med Center.

Kimmy walked them out the door and into the dark hallway of the fifth floor. She keyed open a metal door that revealed a spiral staircase, and stayed downstairs while Robby and Petey began climbing.

The staircase twisted around and around, and in the dark they had to feel their way up the stairs, their hands gripping the rail. Robby laughed in slow motion, and in the narrow stairwell it sounded as though he'd laughed into a microphone. At the top of the stairs, Robby opened a small door that they had to duck to get through, and it was so bright it seemed like they opened a door directly to the sun. For a few seconds neither of them could see. Petey covered his eyes, and when they finally adjusted to the light he felt dizzy. He steadied himself. He was in the middle of the Med Center roof, high above Bridgeport. Because of the height of the rooftop, he was unable to locate himself among any other building. He looked up at the sun to figure out the direction, but it was straight above them.

"Where the fuck are we?" Petey said, and Robby laughed. The rooftop was covered with pebbles, and beneath them, a sheet of plastic. Petey started walking to the roof's edge. He was thinking of the pebbles. They shifted under his footsteps, and it felt as though he were stepping on round and living things.

"Wait up," Robby said. He stopped to relight the joint that had died. There were blue-tip matches in his shirt pocket, and he struck one against the zipper of his pants. He pulled deep and hard from the joint and a seed popped and shot something in his eye. "Fuck!" he said, and Petey waited while Robby rubbed his eye.

Over the shifting pebbles, they plodded to the ledge of the building, and Robby held the joint out to Petey.

"Take this, Petey," he said. "I'm gonna piss on Thirty-second Street."

Petey took the joint but didn't puff on it. Robby unzipped his pants and leaned against the low wall of the rooftop's edge and started pissing.

"Holy shit, Petey," he said. "I'm pissing two streams."

Slowly, Petey looked over the edge, laughing, and, sure enough, Robby was pissing two streams, left and right, like a capital *V.*

That's when Petey realized Robby was pissing onto Wallace Avenue, because there was the Hotdog Hallway across the street. Petey stopped laughing and backed up from the ledge.

When Robby finished, he took the joint from Petey, who'd let it die in the pinch of his thumb and finger. "Did you see that, Petey?" he said. "I'm over there pissing, and it was coming out in two streams, like I had two dicks." He laughed.

"C'mon, Petey," Robby said. "Let's go back to Kimmy's."

But Petey sat down with his back against the ledge where, in all of the world, only Robby Pecca could see him, but it seemed as though maybe Rosalie could see him, too. Petey wondered if boys in Italy smoked dope and pissed off rooftops. He thought about Rosalie's eyes, how green and pretty they were, and felt as though he were the one who had pissed and that Rosalie had seen him with those eyes.

"That was Wallace, Robby," Petey said.

"What was Wallace?" Robby said.

"Wallace," Petey said. "You pissed on Wallace, not Thirty-second Street."

"What the fuck are you talking about?" Robby said.

"Never mind," Petey said.

"You're fucking stoned, man," is what Robby said.

"Go on without me," Petey said.

"What the fuck," Robby said.

Petey stayed on the roof for an hour, until he felt his skin begin to burn from the sun. When he finally stood to return home, he stumbled, bracing himself against the ledge of the roof until the dizziness passed. It smelled like piss. On his way through the dark, twisted stairwell, and the brown hallways of the Med Center apartments, as he walked up Wallace Avenue across the street from the Hotdog Hallway, and until he reached his doorstep, everything smelled of human piss—the sidewalk, the street, the air, his clothes, his skin.

The summer of 1974 was as hot as the winter had been cold, and the worst of the summer's heat and humidity was packed into the last two weeks of July. Inside the Bellapani and Calabrese apartments, there was no relief. On the porch, though, at least in the mornings, there was shade. Sometimes a breeze even whispered its way to their doorsteps. Rosalie had started working three afternoons a week at the Hotdog Hallway, but on mornings, at least until the afternoon sun began to blast away at Bridgeport, she sat on the porch with Petey.

On one afternoon, in the middle of those torrid days of late

July, Petey and Robby Pecca and Davy Stewart were pitching nickels on the Med Center sidewalk, where there was still shade. Ray Ray was there, too. He was long and lanky, an eighteen-year-old with the face of a man. Petey had just tossed a nickel on the line and it bridged the two squares of cement—the grand slam of pitching nickels. He picked up twelve nickels. They were so scuffed and scratched they clicked in his hand like metal washers. Petey had just under three dollars in nickels in his hand when a woman on crutches came out of the Med Center. She walked carefully, slowly, as though she'd never been on crutches before, and at the sound of the approaching 44 Wallace-Racine bus, she looked over her shoulder and hobbled as quickly as she could to catch it at the corner.

Ray Ray was preparing to start another round of nickels when Robby Pecca looked up at the bus, which made Ray Ray look up, too, and then Davy and Petey. In the back of the bus a black man's elbow poked out, holding the window open at the bottom. His head nodded and rocked when the bus started up, and Robby said, "Come on, there's a fuckin' nigger sleeping on the bus!"

When the bus pulled away, Robby threw his nickels against the wall of the Med Center and started running along the sidewalk behind it. Ray Ray threw his nickels down, too, and started running after Robby. Davy looked back at Petey as if he wasn't sure what to do, and then started running, too, but slower.

Petey stayed with the nickels. He watched the three of them run north toward Thirty-first Street. Mid way down the block, rills of heat cushioned Morrissey's Roofing Company. Petey's mother used to say there was a halo over Morrissey's. Ray Ray slowed down at the roofing company, but Robby caught up with the bus at the red light on Thirty-first Street. He stood in the doorway of the Wallace Newspaper office until the light from the cross street turned yellow. He ran to the bus, then slowly lifted the bottom ledge of the big window. Holding it in his hands, he jumped into the air with it, and slammed it on the sleeping man's arm. The black man's arm bounced like rubber, and from a block away, Petey heard the man scream. Ray Ray pointed at the bus and laughed, and Davy looked back at Petey.

Robby ran toward Parnell Street through the alley next to the newspaper office, and Ray Ray and Davy cut east through the gangway near Morrissey's.

Petey wanted to run, too, but no place in the world seemed far enough away. If he could have snapped his fingers and traveled to a place a full world away it would not have been far enough to escape the furious and silent screaming in his head. Across the street from the Med Center, he caught a pissy whiff of beer-soaked wood and ancient smoke from the open door of the Redwood Lounge—and his throat burned with gorge.

Inside the Hotdog Hallway, Mrs. Calabrese wiped the counter while Gina swept the back room. Petey was glad that Rosalie was not working. Since it wasn't busy, she might have been standing in the doorway. She might have seen what Robby did, and heard him say, "C'mon, there's a fuckin' nigger sleeping on the bus." He was glad she had not seen the man's arm bounce like brown rubber. He wondered if Rosalie knew she'd moved to a place where men are awakened sometimes by the sound of their own arms breaking.

When he reached home, Petey knelt in front of the toilet bowl and let spill the rising gorge.

On the last day of July, it was already a hundred degrees at ten o'clock in the morning. The fans in the front windows of Petey's apartment faced outside, because Mr. Bellapani swore that it was a better way to cool a house than facing them indoors.

"I'm not so sure my father knows what he's talking about with this fan business," Petey told Rosalie two weeks earlier. "It's like two hundred degrees in my house, right now."

Rosalie had laughed. She wondered if Mr. Bellapani had discussed the method with her father, for Mr. Calabrese's fans faced outside as well. Rosalie had wondered if her father had fallen for something untrue, and for a moment she felt sad for him.

When he heard Rosalie's footsteps on the stairway above his room, Petey played one of the Billy Joel albums. He wanted "Scenes from an Italian Restaurant" to be playing while they were out in front. When he opened the front door, he found Rosalie leaning against the railing of the porch in a sundress.

Until he saw her there, he hadn't realized he'd never seen her arms before. Even on the hottest of days, she'd always worn long sleeves, but today the sundress bared her arms. They were darker than his, but lighter than her own face and legs.

The first thing to say to Rosalie was always the hardest. Since the day he met her, Petey felt that all he had to do was say too much with his eyes and she'd look away or fly up the stairs in the time it took you to blink. What he wanted to say was that the dress was perfect. It was yellow and green and smart, and Petey thought Rosalie should wear it every day.

At first he didn't know where to sit, he was so used to Rosalie sitting on the step in front of her door. He settled, finally, on his own step. Rosalie didn't lean so much as bounce against the railing. She was rubbing her hand up and down the length of her right arm.

"Is something wrong?" Petey asked.

"No," she answered. "Why?"

"You seem nervous."

"I'm OK," she said.

He could not see her right arm clearly from where he sat, but he thought he saw a flash of something dark on it. A dark spot, like a stain, or a burn.

"Did you hurt yourself?" he asked.

"No," she said.

"Did something happen?" Petey asked, and he began to feel as though he'd already said too much.

"No. What do you mean? No," Rosalie said, and she turned so he couldn't see her arm. "No."

"Your arm," Petey said. "I thought you might've burned yourself at the Hotdog Hallway or something."

"No," Rosalie said. "I'm fine. I have to go." She ran up the stairs, still rubbing her arm.

In her apartment, even Rosalie cringed at the sound of the door she slammed. She had not meant for it to bang so loudly. She went to her bedroom where the hot, damp air hung heavily. She walked through it and sat on her bed, facing the brick wall of the house next door. The window was closed, but even through the glass, she could feel the heat thrown by the bricks of the building next door.

Rosalie went to the dining room and took a chair from the table to set at the front window. She sat inches from the window and turned the fan around so that muggy air rushed at her face. Music whispered through the hum of the fan.

> *A bottle of red, Mmmm, a bottle of white.*
> *Whatever kind of mood you're in tonight.*
> *We'll get a table near the street,*
> *In our old familiar place,*
> *You and I, face to face…*

Rosalie looked at the brown dots that ran the length of her arm, tracing them with her fingers. She stood, then, and walked into her parents' bedroom. Against the wall, on her mother's side of the bed, a full-length swivel mirror rested on its wooden feet. Rosalie angled it so that she could see her body, but not her face. She looked at the reflection of her arm, traced the marks with her left hand. She considered how the mirror reversed things. She re-adjusted the mirror so that she could see her face. The green of the sundress set off something in her eyes. They looked greener somehow. Rosalie left her parents' room, and walked toward the hallway.

She opened the door and began her walk downstairs. The

music seemed to be coming from an open door, but she was still uncertain whether Petey was there. When she reached the threshold she saw him, still sitting on the step in front of his door. He held a glass of lemonade in his hands, and there was another at his side.

"I'm sorry if I said something," Petey said.

Rosalie took the spot she'd taken earlier. She leaned against the railing, her right arm behind her back.

"I brought you a lemonade," Petey said, and he handed her the glass at his side.

Rosalie felt the tang of the lemonade in her jaw before she accepted the glass from Petey, and maybe it was that, or Billy Joel, or the fact that June had passed, and now July would pass as well, and soon all of summer would be gone, or maybe it was just that the porch was the only thing that Rosalie liked about this new place, and she was happy that Petey was still there. It was all of it, and the lemonade, too, that made Rosalie feel it would be OK if she told Petey everything, and even showed him her arm. It would be good, she thought, to have something of her own to say.

Rosalie reached her left hand toward Petey and wrapped her fingers around the cool, sweating glass, thanking him. She sipped it, and set it on her step before leaning against the railing.

They were quiet for a moment before Rosalie pulled her right arm from behind her back. The imprint of the twisted iron rail had reddened on her palm. She looked at it, and dropped her arm at her side.

"It's a birthmark," Rosalie said.

"On your arm?" Petey asked.

"Yes. It's a birthmark and I hate it," Rosalie said, and started rubbing her arm again. "My mother thinks it's a rose, but it's gross and lumpy and brown and I hate it." It was the longest sentence Petey thought he'd ever heard.

"Was it there when you were born?" Petey asked.

Rosalie looked at him.

"Yes. It's a birthmark," she said.

It sounded very American to hear Rosalie say that.

"It'll be there when I die, too," she added.

Petey made the connection then, between her name and the rose on her arm. He wondered if it had been a rose at the moment of her birth. He thought of Mr. and Mrs. Calabrese, on the day of their daughter's birth, looking at the flower on her tiny arm. He imagined they had planned to give her some other name, but in the moment of seeing the sign of the rose, had changed their minds, and agreed on the name by which she would forever be known. A baby with a rose on her arm had been given to them, and there was little else to do with such a miracle than to call her Rosalie. Or had it become a rose as she grew? Petey wondered. Had she been named after the rose, or had the rose grown to fit her name? Would it be more or less of a rose as the baby's arm became a girl's arm?

Petey wanted to see the rose. He wanted her to stop hiding it from him, and he wanted her to stop trying to erase it. He wanted her to stop moving so that he could look at the rose. He wondered if he would be able to see the rose, or would he see only ugly brown spots, as Rosalie did? He would find the rose on her arm, he decided. He would find it for Rosalie. Even if it was hard to see, he'd find it there, and he was certain it would be beautiful. He wanted to say this to Rosalie even before seeing her arm, but was afraid it might make her leave. Instead, he told her what he'd wanted to say earlier.

"You look nice," he said.

And when she smiled, Petey Bellapani asked Rosalie Calabrese if he could see the rose on her arm, as if it were a thing that belonged to her.

"May I see your rose?" he said.

In the silence that followed, Rosalie seemed to consider his request. Petey wondered if anyone had ever asked this before, or if anyone outside her family even knew she had one.

Rosalie stopped rubbing her arm, still protecting what small part of the rose she could; but after a moment she allowed

her left hand to drop from it. She sat in her old seat then, at
her doorstep, holding her lemonade and touching her knee to
his. Petey still wasn't sure she'd let him see the rose, but after
a few minutes, she set her glass down and held her arm above
his knee.

Petey didn't look immediately; he was afraid she might pull
her arm away, or run up the stairs if he did. And it was not
lost on him that her knee was bare, dark and bare, and that it
touched him.

He waited until Rosalie looked up at him, until he saw her
olive eyes again, and it seemed to him as though she held contact
with his eyes for a long time, much longer than ever before.
Petey opened his fingers on his lap, then, and Rosalie set her
hand, cool and wet from the lemonade, onto Petey's palm. He
waited for her to look at him, as if to ask again.

There was no denying it was a rose. Long, thin stem and
all. Tight brown dots climbed from the well of her palm upward,
forming a leaf across her forearm. Just below her elbow there
was a knobby deviation in the stem, and another leaf began at
the bend of her arm. A thorn grew from the stem just above that
leaf, and another grew from the delicate rise of her bicep.

It was a rose, a perfect rose, and Petey marveled at its perfect
thorns. He imagined the thorns actually causing Rosalie pain.
He wanted to touch them. He looked up at her, but she looked
away, as if she knew that he wanted to touch her arm. Petey felt
her fingers unfold from their lazy curl, as if Rosalie was saying
Yes to the question Petey had not asked. He put his finger to
the white of her palm, and moved slowly to her wrist, where
he touched the lowest part of the stem. He didn't feel the color
raised on her skin. He closed his eyes to see if he could feel the
rose with his eyes shut, and though he didn't feel the mark of
her birth, he knew he was touching something more than the
skin of a girl.

It seemed to Petey, as his finger moved up her arm, that he
could feel the path of it on his own arm as well. He wondered
if its trace would become a remembered thing, if she would feel

Petey's fingers on her arm even after she went upstairs. He wondered if she would still feel his fingers there tomorrow.

As Petey traced the stem to the crook of her arm, Rosalie looked at his carelessly combed hair, and for a second she thought she might reach toward him to comb it with her fingers. Her fingers were thin enough to comb with. She fought against the urge to move toward him. She was still looking at him when he raised his eyes to her again.

Petey touched the thorns. He ran his fingers along each of their points. He thought of an actual rose, how you knew better than to touch the tips of real thorns, but how you wanted to touch them anyway, because it seemed like when you looked at them they were the sharpest things in all the world. Petey moved his finger along the stem to the middle of Rosalie's upper arm, and he looked at her shoulder. He wondered if there was a flower to the rose. There must be. It seemed as though Rosalie herself depended upon there being a flower. Somewhere beyond the strap of her sundress, Petey thought, was the rest of the rose. He slid his fingers back to Rosalie's wrist, then, and held her hand in both of his.

"Is the flower on your shoulder?" Petey asked.

Rosalie said nothing. She looked into Petey's eyes and brought her left hand to her shoulder. She shaped her dark fingers into a kind of protective bowl over her tiny breast, and inched the strap of her sundress down to reveal the rest of the flower.

The cup of the rose was full, and on the inside of her shoulder the tips of the petals turned inward. It had not yet opened. It was a flower on the verge of itself. The birthmark didn't end at the flower, though; Petey could see there was more. Rosalie kept her middle finger where it held the strap of her sundress, and used her pinky to slide down the low curve of the arm of the dress so that the rest of the flower was revealed. And in that space, the space that would one day become the outside arc of woman's breast, a single petal of a rose was falling.

The petal is falling, Petey thought. It will always be falling.

The logic of the rose did not occur to Petey then, and although she had seen the rose a thousand times, nor did it occur to Rosalie. Neither of them considered the paradox that a petal was falling from a rose whose flower had yet to open.

After she revealed the falling petal, Rosalie kept her hand where it held the strap aside, like the curtain to an offering. She looked down at her fingers, and the fact of the sundress surprised her. Before that morning, she had never even tried a sundress on. She remembered the first time she'd seen one. She thought there was nothing more beautiful in the world. It was a thing she'd never imagined wearing. As she stood in front of her mother's mirror that morning, she'd argued with herself over her sister's old sundress or a T-shirt and shorts, and a dozen times she changed her mind. On and off she slipped the sundress, on and off the T-shirt. When she finally settled on the dress, she wondered if she would have the courage to sit on the porch. She'd sat at the edge of her mother's bed, angling herself so that the mirror could see only the left side of her body.

A thousand times Rosalie had cursed the ugly brown spots on her arm, and a thousand times convinced herself that a boy would never see the rose. What boy would ever love her so deeply that she would show him the rose? That very morning she'd tried to imagine a boy kissing her. In her diary she had written that if a boy ever kissed her it would have to be winter. It would be cold and she would be covered with a sweater and jacket, and the boy would not know about the rose. She thought she would have to fool a boy in order to be kissed. And after the kiss she would have a secret to keep if they were ever to kiss again.

But on the porch it was nearly August in a very warm place, and she sat next to a boy with brown eyes who was holding her hand, and it seemed to Rosalie as though she sat there with more than just her hand in his. It seemed, in fact, that he had everything of hers in his hands, and that a kiss was possible.

She thought she might let Petey kiss her then if he wanted.

She thought that if he moved his finger back up the rose and toward her shoulder she might let him. Petey had stopped tracing the rose at the middle of her arm, but Rosalie thought that if he wanted to continue to where the tips of the petals curved in at the top, she would allow such a tracing. If he wanted even to follow the path of the falling petal she would let him.

Rosalie wondered what he would say now. Nothing, she hoped. She hoped he would return her arm to her lap, maybe offer her the glass of lemonade again, but she didn't want him to speak. She didn't think this could end in the right way. Petey would say something and she'd be sorry, sorry her family had ever moved here, sorry it was hot, sorry she had worn a stupid sundress, and sorry she'd shown a boy her ugly arm. And even if Petey didn't say something stupid—even if it was nice, the thing he might say—she hoped he wouldn't say it at all.

And though it is true that Bridgeport, and perhaps the whole world, was filled with boys who wouldn't know what to do with a girl with a rose on her arm, Petey knew that a flower had been shared with him. He felt as though he'd been chosen. And as he sat there with Rosalie's hand in his, Petey wondered if she would let him kiss her. He thought it was possible that she might even lean toward him and kiss him. If she did, he'd let her. Petey thought, then, of Debbie Vaccaro and Mikey Rico leaning against the bricks of Bernie's, how she'd pressed her hips against Rico and kissed him. There hadn't been much to that kiss, after all, Petey thought. His first kiss would not be like that. It wouldn't happen on a corner and smoke would not come out of his mouth.

And if Rosalie had said I love you just then, Petey would have returned those same words to her. She was dark and thin and sad, and she had been named after a rose, and Petey Bellapani felt he might love her.

Without looking away from Rosalie's arm, Petey held her hand in his, and he was no longer afraid of saying something that would make her run away. He took in all of the rose of Rosalie, and he felt there could be no wrong thing to say. It seemed as though he had the power to say the perfect thing, the power even to fix things, to make the heat go away if he pleased, to bring a sweetness to fetid air. To heal. And at the sound of the 44-Wallace-Racine bus passing, Petey looked up to find Rosalie gazing at the rose on her arm, and he wondered what it looked like from above–not only the rose, he wondered what everything looked like from above: the guys pitching nickels in front of the Med Center, a boy pissing off its roof, a bakery fire. He wondered what a softball game looked like from above. What it looked like to see someone crush a man's arm.

He also wondered what a boy and a girl looked like, sitting on the porch, the girl's arm in the boy's hands, and in that moment it occurred to him that Rosalie's birthmark could have been anything. It could have been anything between a smudge of brown spots and a beautiful flower.

When Rosalie looked up, Petey set her arm across her own lap as gently as if he were placing an infant there. Only then did she take her hand from her chest and let her shoulder strap return to its natural place. She smoothed her dress over her legs.

Petey reached for Rosalie's lemonade and placed the still-cool glass in her hand so that she had something to hold. He moved across the porch to sit against the black iron railing that climbed the stairs to his left, while Rosalie sat against the railing on her side. She held the glass of lemonade in both hands and allowed Petey to see her arm from across the porch. She did not try to hide or erase the rose.

After a few minutes passed, Petey raised the glass of lemonade to his lips, and it seemed to Rosalie that she could taste what Petey did, the cool and wet and tang of the lemonade swirling from the glass into his mouth.

He set his drink on the cement and looked into Rosalie's eyes. He wanted her to know everything. He wanted her to know that her eyes were the greenest things in all of Bridgeport. He wanted her to know that the thing on her arm was not a smudge of brown spots, there was definitely a rose there, and he wanted her to know that it was beautiful and that he thought she should wear sundresses every day and he hoped it would never be cold again, but that even if it was cold again, she should still consider wearing a sundress.

How much time would it take, Petey wondered, to tell Rosalie everything? And how much time remained? He hoped there was time enough to tell her everything, and on the chance there wasn't, he said the one thing that couldn't wait.

"It's a rose," he said. "It could've been a million other things."

# The Thing About Swing

Against the dark Sunday sky the Suds-All-Night Laundromat was so bright it seemed proud of itself. Painted on a glass panel of the building, a sleepy-eyed cartoon lady poured a box of detergent into a washing machine. Suds spilled over the sides. Through the glass Danny could see the place was empty.

He banged his basket through the double doors and heard the hum of two, maybe three, washing machines. Only one other person, he thought. She must've slipped out for a minute. Or *he*. Past the island of washers the big folding table was empty, so Danny hurried to his left and bounced his laundry basket on it. He set to work with a sport-like intensity.

Danny no longer fumbled like a freshman through the calm and storm of laundering, the ninety-minute negotiation of turf and time. He had a system. He put his jacket at the edge of the table to reserve the space for folding his clothes, and carried his basket to the washers, where he selected three in a row—two for colors, one for whites. He poured in soap powder, slipped quarters into the coin slots, and pushed in the plates to start the machines; and as the drums filled with water, he sorted and tossed clothes with the speed and confidence that come from knowing what the hell you're doing. Whites, colors, colors, whites...

He shut the lids of the washers and returned to the folding table across from dryers one, two, and three across the aisle. He shaped his hand into a pistol, and muttered, "Boom, boom, boom," by which poetry he laid secret claim to the three dryers. He imagined his clothes rising and falling in ambient motion behind the glass doors, and he moved his head in the circles he imagined.

He leaned against the back of his chair and sighed deeply at his efficiency and fortune; an empty Laundromat, three open dryers right there in front of him—why, he'd be back on campus in record time. It was probably, what? Ten-twenty? Danny looked at the clock above the dryers, saw the short hand for the hour, the long for the minute, and the quick for the second, but he never registered the exact time, for the scope of his vision had shifted just enough for him to realize he was no longer alone. To his right were the sandaled feet, the corduroyed legs, and one thinly sweatered shoulder of a girl. She sat in a chair along the north wall of windows. Danny's laundry basket obstructed the view of her face. Must have left to get more quarters, Danny thought.

Which was exactly the case. Just minutes before, as Danny walked toward the Laundromat, the girl had been picking through a mess of coins buried in the glove compartment of her car. She had seen him rest his tub of laundry on his hip to open the door. When she reentered the Suds-All-Night, she'd settled into her chair at the window and watched him move, quickly, but with a kind of ease, she'd thought, from machine to machine, slotting coins, pushing levers, sorting clothes. When he finally sat down after that initial rush, she had this to think as well: The boy was rather tall.

The girl pulled a novel from her backpack and opened it to a page she'd marked with a folded corner. She stretched her legs out, crossed them at her feet, and began to read—which is why she didn't see Danny rise from his chair to open, slightly and possessively, the doors of the dryers across from him. Danny thought what he always thought when he opened the round doors of the dryers: They're like submarine doors.

He returned to his chair and looked the girl's way; she was reading a novel. He leaned forward to see its title but found the distance too great. It reminded him, though, of his own book. He slid back in his chair and reached into his jacket for Walker Percy's *Love in the Ruins*—required reading for Philosophy 271.

He flipped to his bookmarked page and, for the third time that day, read the first paragraph on page 104:

> *Later, lust gave way to sorrow and I prayed, arms stretched out like a Mexican, tears streaming down my face. Dear God, I can see it now, why can't I see it other times, that it is you I love in the beauty of the world and in all the lovely girls and dear good friends, and it is pilgrims we are, wayfarers on a journey, and not pigs, nor angels.*

Just as he'd begun to reflect upon this passage and its importance to what he'd read so far, the final spin of a washing machine whistled and rumbled to a stop. The girl set her book on the chair next to her and paused. She seemed to be listening for something. Seconds later, another machine whirred to the end of its cycle, and the girl rose from her seat and walked to the washers.

Pretty well dressed for laundry day, Danny thought. Her pants were a tightly ribbed tan corduroy; her sweater was thin and powder blue. She moved easily, slenderly, transferring the contents of the first washer as if she weren't concerned about time. When she was done she carried her basket in Danny's direction.

Danny lowered his head to his book. He figured she was on her way past him, toward the second bank of dryers where she might find two or three that had clearly not been reserved, but she stopped instead at the dryers in front of him. She opened the door to number three and tossed in her clothes.

Two things came to Danny's mind then: She's pretty tall, was the first of them. Probably played basketball. Or volleyball. And the second thing to cross his mind was *Shit,* for she'd stolen one of his dryers, and for the first time since entering the Suds-All-Night, his heart raced.

The girl closed the door to dryer number three, not bothering to load it with quarters, and returned to the washers for her second load.

Danny watched from the corner of his eye and considered Plan B. Assuming the girl had designs on dryers three and four, he figured he'd use one and two, and since he'd need a third dryer, maybe he'd use one from the bank of machines farther down.

When the girl returned to Danny's area, though, she stopped in front of number one and began to unload her basket. Something like a question mark wrinkled into Danny's brow. He set his novel on his lap and crossed his arms. Number one? he thought. Why would she separate her dryers from each other like that? It made no sense. The girl shut the doors to dryers one and three.

Maybe she's never been to the Suds-All-Night before, Danny thought. Maybe she's never been to any Laundromat. Maybe the washing machine in her apartment just broke down and she had to come here to do her laundry, and maybe that's why she doesn't know what the hell she's doing.

The possibility of the girl's innocence settled Danny, and against her skimpy logic he soothed himself with the soundness of his own: He had a pocketful of quarters, there were plenty of dryers to go around, and he'd secured the best folding space in the Laundromat. He reached to his left and double-patted the table.

The girl clinked a quarter into dryer number three and turned the knob to register it. She slipped in a second quarter. A third. A fourth. A fifth and a sixth. Seven minutes of drying time per quarter, Danny thought, and with each clink of another coin, the likelihood of her innocence slipped away.

"Forty-two minutes," he said to himself as she turned the knob to settle the sixth coin. Just about right. It didn't square well with innocence. She'd been here before. Similarly, she coined dryer number one, and when the sixth coin fell, the girl pivoted sharply, and as her sandaled feet stepped toward Danny, he knew, from the confidence in her stride, that she was not finished usurping Danny's position at the Suds-All-Night. She was about to claim possession of his folding table as well, and the dukes of his competitive heart rose within.

He looked up slowly, his eyes at her knees as the laundry basket left her fingertips, at her shoulders as the basket sailed through the air, and with every millisecond that passed, every infinitesimal variation in the scope of his sight, he felt a growing need to stand up for himself, so that by the time his eyes had taken in the decorative button on the neck of her sweater, his pressing desire to demand fair treatment had reached a frenzied point beyond which it could not rise without spilling over. The basket thudded on the table.

To his left, was the sibilant whisper of the basket as it slid to the wall. In front of him was the girl, looking in his eyes, smiling. He hadn't expected a smile, and the rigid spirit that had been mounting within him was gone, was replaced by something pacific, and soft, and infinitely lighter. It was an inexplicable and excellent trade, and so quickly had the swap occurred, that it left Danny swooning under the soporific effect of its release. All he could do for a second—though it seemed like many—was look at her. He didn't fix on any single feature—the languid part in her hair, or the blue of her eyes—but he noticed the way the light rolled around her, and how shade moved in the hollows and along the lines of her neck. He was intensely aware of the spaces at which one feature passed into another, the uncertain loci at which they met.

The corners of her smile twitched upward, and then, as if kicked into some higher gear, he felt a skip in his breath and a shift in the cadence of his heart. And the convergence of this shift and skip made him feel as though the contents of his heart had been revealed, as though there were a word balloon above his head that held, just then, a line from page 104 of *Love in the Ruins*: "It is you I love in the beauty of the world." Danny had no history of recalling quotes from novels, but this one came to him with such clarity that he put his finger to his lips for fear he might say the words aloud.

The girl walked to the snack machine that separated the banks of dryers, and as Danny considered her unhurried movement through the place, he thought of how rushed he must have appeared as he went about his own laundering, how blindly he'd kept to his system, how not seeing had become the cost of reckless motion. Immediately and intensely, he felt a prodigal's remorse, as though it were possible he'd wasted as much as a life. What if this very girl had crossed his path on some sunny day as he'd walked across campus? Or what if they'd stood in the same line at the grocery store and he hadn't even looked her way? And if he could pass a girl like this on the street and not see her, then how much else of life had he missed?

In the window of the snack machine, the girl found Danny's reflection. He'd returned to his book, the cover of which was difficult to see in the glass. She thought again, mostly because of the stretch and bend of his legs, and the ease with which his torso cleared the back of the chair, that he really was quite tall. And with this second consideration of his height, she allowed a thought to surface that she'd held off since reentering the Suds-All-Night: He might make a good swing partner.

The first time she'd seen a couple swing was at a party on campus somewhere. It was loud and the place was packed and, without any warning, the music stopped, and it was quiet for a second and then a new song came on. A couple she'd seen sitting on a couch got up and started to swing. There was only a tiny bit of floor space open in the living room, so they kept the dance contained until people began to step back and watch, and inch by inch the room opened up for them, and their swing grew, and the way they moved, the easy, happy, beauty of it—the way they touched hands and smiled at each other, the way they held each other at the hips, let each other go, and spun away to dance their own private dances, and the way each of them knew exactly where the other was all the time, the precise timing of it, the way they swung—it left her with a thrill so strong that it saddened her. She thought she might live her life and never be danced around a floor like that.

And since the day she'd learned she could fulfill her final P.E. requirement with swing dance, she'd secretly been measuring potential partners. On the bus, at the supermarket, in the line for class registration, she found herself looking for guys who were taller than she. And, recently, she'd begun to despair that no one was tall enough anymore. She had considered taking her chances with a random pairing, but decided against it; it was just her luck to be coupled with someone who came to her shoulders, and nothing against short guys, but her thing about swing was this: She longed to be swung. And what if she found someone tall enough in the supermarket, anyway? What then? Would she ask a complete stranger to take a dance class with her?

She began to turn away from the reflection of the boy, when she noticed him raise his eyes from his book and look her way. She wondered if the boy could see her reflection in the glass. She caught herself raising her hand to wave at him, and, at the last second, to disguise her instinct to wave, she pretended to reach for the coin slot, but her hand was empty, so she pulled it back before it reached the machine. There was nothing she wanted from it. Without buying a snack, she turned away from the vending machine and toward her seat. She smiled as she passed the boy, wondering if it was enough for swing that a boy was tall. She worried that tall was maybe not enough. That you needed something more, and she returned to her seat at the window.

It seemed to Danny, as he watched the girl stand at the vending machine, that she'd waved at him through the glass. He looked up as she walked past him, and though it was possible he had missed a thousand other smiles, he didn't miss this one;

he had seen her smile. And as Danny's blue regret washed away, he felt as though he'd been given something. A gift. And he recalled a winter day when he was ten years old. His father had taken him to his first Chicago Bears game, and near the end of the third quarter, a player had thrown a football into the stands to celebrate a touchdown reception. The ball appeared to be headed toward the outstretched hands of any number of fans, but it slipped every grasp, hit the side of a man's neck, knocked someone's beer over, and finally landed on Danny's lap. His father put his hand on top of the ball to mark the completion of its journey, and Danny looked up at his father.

"Can I keep it, Dad?" he said.

His father laughed and mussed his hair.

"You can keep it, Danny Boy," he said.

In the car, Danny's father shook his head and smiled all the way home. "You lucky son of a gun," he said. "Who comes home from a football game with a game football?"

The answer to which question, of course, was Danny, who had, since his early boyhood, a sort of sports-arena luck. In addition to that football, displayed like trophies in his room, were three hockey pucks and nine major-league baseballs—all effortlessly acquired. And though it was a fortune entirely bound by the geography of sport, Danny was unaware of its parameters; which is to say, he simply felt lucky.

And as he sat in the Laundromat, Danny couldn't say how he'd come to recall this day with his father at the Bears game, but he was certain of this: The girl had smiled at him. And with it, he felt she'd given him something like a promise, or a truth he hadn't known before the smile. Something he could touch.

When the girl sat down to her novel, Danny returned to his *Love in the Ruins*. He had barely reached the end of the same paragraph, though, when he heard the first of his own washers complete its cycle. That's me, he thought. He set his book on the chair and walked toward his washers, looking ahead to where the girl sat. As she read, her index finger lay bent across her lips, and the pad of her thumb touched under her chin, and a thought swirled in Danny's head: How much time have we left here?

He opened the lid of the machine, and as he began to peel his whites from the drum, he reflected, briefly, on the phenomenon of centrifugal force as applied to the laundering process. The wet clothes spin away from the center, he reflected, and are forced against the circular wall of the machine. He hadn't the language for pondering this physical force with any greater depth, except that he knew the word centripetal suggested a spinning toward the center. But this, he reflected further, if it were an actual force at all, didn't seem to be a Laundromat phenomenon. He transferred his laundry from the washing machine to his rope-handled tub, and looked toward the girl again.

She wore the colors of sand and sky. At her waist, where these colors met, he followed the sand of her to her feet, and the sky of her to her face, and in that moment she made perfect sense to him. Everything seemed to flow from the core of her. Every line and curve, every color and shape, seemed connected to some inner, impalpable thing; as if living spokes flowed from the hub of her to become eyes and skin and lips and things.

And it was at this consideration of the idea of lips, that the memory of a girl Danny knew from grade school came to him. Her name was Rene, and she must have gone to St. David's with Danny for only a year or so, for he had no other memory of her. They were on a field trip at a children's theater—it was the fourth grade, because Ms. Balich had taken them to the theater—and the play was about to begin. Rene was excited about the production—he remembered that; she was smiling and her eyes were opened wide. Her right leg was crossed over her lap, and her foot rocked in such a way, that on every upswing, her shoe tapped against his leg. Danny didn't move. He looked straight ahead, for fear that if he did anything else, she might stop tapping against him.

Then Rene shifted in her seat, it seemed she wanted to say something to Danny. She uncrossed her legs and tapped him on the wrist, and leaned toward him to whisper, but his right ear, the ear on her side, was bandaged; he'd been hit with a rock while playing at the Wallace Playlot, which was being torn down to make way for houses. Danny was about to shift almost completely around in order to offer his left ear to her, but Rene put her fingers to his cheek to stop him from turning. And the easy way she put her fingertips to his face made Danny feel she was grown up, and his heart pounded against his chest.

Rene brought her face closer to his, and when she began again to say this thing to him, it was nearly into his lips that she said it. She held his face in her hand and she whispered into his lips as though she believed he would hear her best this way, and so aware was Danny of how close her lips were to his own, that even as the words left her mouth he could not recall what they were; he had only his eyes to help him make sense of the sounds. He could only look into her lips and at the skin of her cheeks, and see the tiniest curved lines form at the corners of her mouth as she spoke, and at the moment of the whispering, he thought: This is it. This is what before a kiss must feel like.

And as he grew, on those occasions when someone asked him to tell the story of his first kiss, this is the story that came to mind, though never the story he told.

After pouring his clothes into the dryer and loading the slot with quarters, Danny had barely returned to his seat when another of his washers clicked to a stop. He walked to the machines and set his basket on the one to his left so that, as he transferred his clothes, he might look in the girl's direction. She appeared to be reading, but as they each seemed legitimately occupied—he with the transfer of clothes, and she with her reading—they secretly alternated glances at each other.

As Danny leaned into the machine, the girl decided that there was more to him than height. There was definitely a kind of grace to him, and a precision—traits she thought might have some value in swing.

Danny completed the transfer of clothes, and peered into the machine to make certain it was empty. A sock was stuck against the side of the washer. He peeled it off, tossed it into his basket, and headed toward dryer number four. He decided then, that when the time came to dry his final basket of clothes, he wouldn't use a third dryer after all. He'd distribute his final basket among dryers two and four instead. It would take longer for the clothes to dry that way, but there was no longer a reason to hurry.

Something clinked against the glass door of one of the girl's dryers. A buckle from her overalls, perhaps. He opened the door to dryer four, emptied his tub of laundry into it, and twisted the knob to register his quarters. The moment the sound of heat rushed through the machine, his final washer stopped, completing the shift of sound from the north end to the center of the Laundromat, where the first bank of dryers was running at full throttle.

As Danny reached his washer, the girl set down her book and slid back in her chair. She caught Danny's eye again. Each of them feeling the contact was justified because of the change in the sound of the place. They smiled.

As Danny began emptying his final load from the drum of the washer, the girl's smile remained before him. He blinked twice, and her smiling face returned. It was like looking into the sun and then looking away. Yes. She had something like the sun within her. In spite of the great brightness of the Suds-All-Night, he felt that if she opened the door and walked out just then, it was possible the light might go with her, and there would remain scarcely enough by which to read, and if she left just then, it was possible, as well, Danny thought, that the night might reverse itself and day prevail. And Danny was afraid of the darkness she would leave behind.

He reached into the washer and pulled at a pair of jeans. They were twisted around a sweatshirt. He untangled them, and removed a pair of boxers from the wall of the machine, felt the tug of the shorts from dozens of tiny drain holes. He lifted his basket, and as he walked toward the dryers, his back to the girl, he felt as though he were walking from silence into sound.

He called upon her image again, and like something known, her face registered perfectly in his mind, and it worried him to recall her so clearly.

These were things about the girl that Danny could not have known:

Because he could not make out small letters from across a room, he did not know she was reading a book called *Love in the Time of Cholera*, rereading it, actually, because of a quote she'd remembered. She never recalled the line exactly, but she'd thought of it nearly every day since she'd read it two years before: Already lost in the mists of death, she moved the pieces without love. Though it was a line of great sadness, she had a breathing faith in its truth, and in the lesson for living it implied.

And there was this: She'd been called Rain once, on mistake, and she secretly loved the name.

This also he could not have known: when she was a child in the autumn of sixth grade, she came upon an injured pigeon on her way to school. She approached it slowly, making warbling, throaty, soothing sounds. It surprised her that she could produce a sound so like the coo of a pigeon. She came within inches of the bird, which didn't scurry away or flinch at the reach of her arm; it seemed, rather, to expect carriage and tending. She set it delicately in her jacket pocket so that it faced forward, and wondered if, in the history of the world, a pigeon had ever been in a girl's pocket. She brushed the nape of the bird's neck with her thumb, and for many years afterward, she would recall its softness. She'd often find herself touching the skin under her own chin, or other soft things, with her thumb.

It is fair to say that Rain had a crush on the world. On pencils with dark, gritty lead. On Chicago Septembers and magnets. On an old Italian woman she'd passed on the street once; she wanted to touch her. She had a crush on mornings, too. Some nights she got so excited about waking up the next day that it wasn't until morning that she finally fell asleep. She was never far from a broken heart because of the things she loved, but it was worth the crush of them.

There were many things about the girl that Danny could not have known, but if he'd had the ability to see into what kind of woman a little girl might become, he might have known this: that the clothes in dryers number one and three, belonged to a woman named Rene.

Danny carried his final tub of clothes to the silver machines that had been tumbling for several minutes on the strength of his quarters, and as he approached the seat next to his, he glanced at pages 104 and 105 of his novel. The bend of the paperback reminded him of a child's drawing of birds. Little *m*'s in the sky.

He stood at dryer three, with his final basket of wet laundry resting on his hip, his fingers on the handle, and, glancing at the girl who sat at the window, he again recalled the day his fourth grade class attended the children's theater, and he wished he'd have put his fingers to Rene's cheeks. He wished he'd have looked her in the eyes and kissed her whispering lips.

And while Danny stared at the spin and tumble of the clothes, his lips nearly took the shape of a kiss, and this momentary change in the contour of his lips, along with the tinny clink of a buckle against metal, urged him to open the door to dryer three. The drum of the machine barely stopped turning as he dumped in the last of his clothes. He shut the door and felt the pull of the magnetic lock, the tug and click of the door as it snapped shut.

He pressed the button to restart the dryer and looked at the girl, and it was only then—as the rumble of the machine resumed—that he realized the dryer was not his at all, but hers.

He reached out his hand and touched the thick window of the door, felt the warmth of the machine, the faint thump of the girl's sweater against the glass, and there seemed to be a slower motion to the tumble of clothes, a turn in the music of the machine. He stood there with his eyes closed and listened to the dryer, while, across the Laundromat, a girl named Rene looked at him.

She couldn't be sure, but it seemed as though the boy had just closed the door of her dryer, and if it was her dryer he'd closed, it also seemed that he might have emptied his basket of laundry into it.

She set her novel on the seat next to her and began to walk toward him. The tall boy stared into dryer three, and two things were clear as Rene came closer: first, that the look on his face was unquestionably the look of a boy who had mistakenly dumped his wet clothes into the working dryer of a stranger; and second, that there was something familiar about him, a certainty in his face. Had she taken a class with him, or met him on campus somewhere? Maybe he worked in the bookstore or the café. What did not occur to her, was that a girl could not forget the face of a boy into whose lips she once had whispered.

She was steps away from Danny when she saw, through the door of dryer number three, someone else's clothes tumbling with hers. Was it possible, she wondered, for a boy to accidentally ask a girl to dance? And she smiled, because this is what she felt he'd done.

She stopped, and Danny spoke first.

"I, uh, dumped my clothes into yours," he said.

"Yes, I thought you might have," she said. It seemed to Danny that she was holding back a smile.

"It was an accident," he said.

"Well, it's a funny way to meet a girl," she said.

She was smiling. Curved lines appeared at the corners of her mouth, perfect parentheses.

"My name is Danny," he said.

"Rene," she said.

"I'm sorry?" Danny said.

"It's OK," she said.

"No, what I mean is that I'm not sure I heard your name right," he said.

"Oh," she said. "Rene."

And Danny smiled. He smiled because he could see then what had become of a little girl, a girl he would have kissed if he'd been given the chance to go back in time. He smiled then because he felt lucky.  As if he had a seat just behind the glass at a Blackhawks game, and two players had attacked a puck at the same time, and with such perfect force, that the puck left the rink and was flipping toward Danny in slow motion.

"Why are you smiling?" Rene said, and she could not help smiling herself.

"Why are you smiling?" Danny returned.

"Well, I was just thinking we'll have to sort our clothes," she said.  "And I think that's funny, to sort clothes with someone you've never met.  Now, why were you smiling?"

"I was thinking almost the same thing," Danny said.  "I was thinking how funny it was to sort clothes with someone I haven't seen since the fourth grade."

Rene smiled again, and wrinkled her eyes.  She smiled because she had been remembered, and she wrinkled her eyes because she wondered at the exact memory.

"You can wait here with me while they dry, if you'd like," Danny said. He nodded toward the seat next to him, and Rene, still smiling, sat down. Danny picked up his book and put it on the table. When he looked back at her, she was looking at him.

"Fourth grade." Rene said. "St. David's. I went to a school called St. David's that year."

"Yes," Danny said. "So did I."

They were quiet for a moment as they looked at the sluggish tumbling of their clothes behind the glass door, each of them comforted at the sight of something familiar, and excited at the sight of something not.

A sleeve of Rene's orange sweater brushed against the glass, and as the rest of the clothes danced behind it, the arm of the sweater lingered there a moment longer than either Danny or Rene had expected it to.  Rene thought it was like a wave, as if her sweater were waving at them. Danny thought so, too. He felt that the sweater was saying hello, and he felt he should say something to keep from waving back. And Rene thought that if

Danny hadn't said something just then, she might have waved back, too.

"I almost kissed you once," Danny said.

"Yes," Rene said. "You almost did."

Billy Lombardo began writing as a poet in the Chicago slam poetry scene. His fiction has appeared in such publications as *StoryQuarterly, Other Voices, Cicada,* and the *Bryant Literary Revew.* He teaches fiction and directs the Service Learning Program at The Latin School of Chicago, where he also serves as the faculty sponsor for *Polyphony H.S.*, a new national literary magazine for high-school writers. A graduate of Loyola University, and a lifelong resident of the Chicago area, Billy now lives in Forest Park with his wife, Elisa, a singer/songwriter, and his sons, Seth and Kane. Billy writes for *The Forest Park Post* and can be reached through his website, www.billylombardo.com.